fragments of truth

PIERCED HEARTS
BOOK THREE

VIOLET HAZE

Cover by Designs by Dana
Stoked Publishing House

ISBN-13: 978-1-7355302-4-6
First Edition: September 2025

blurb

I thought I'd finally moved on from Evan Pierce. After years of being his secret, I was ready to build something real with Jake—a man who actually wanted to be seen with me.

Jake is everything Evan isn't: reliable, honest, and unafraid to fight for what he wants. With him, I don't have to wonder where I stand or wait for scraps of attention.

But then Evan shows up at my door, finally ready to say the words I've been waiting to hear. Now he wants to fight for us, claiming he was wrong to let me go.

I'm caught between the man who taught me I deserve better and the man I haven't stopped loving.

How do you choose between the love you've always wanted and the love you know you deserve?

spoiler alert!

Please be aware, while this story may be read as a standalone, reading *Fragments of Us* and *Fragments of Hope* first is best!

This novel will also continue many storylines from the first two books. Unless you don't mind being lost at first as to who's who, or ruining the ending of the previous novels, my recommendation is that you get to know everyone from the beginning!

Happy Reading! :)

ONE

AFTER STEFAN DIED, MY WHOLE WORLD FELL APART.

I wish that was an exaggeration, but it isn't.

The night he died, Yvette screamed at me and Evan, calling us disgusting and saying it was our fault he died, because he'd seen us kissing.

First, when had he seen us kissing? Evan hadn't kissed me at that party, although he had leaned in pretty close to my face to say something. We wouldn't have dared to do something as stupid as kiss at a family party before telling his brother as well as everybody else about us. Of course, Yvette's little outburst pretty much took care of announcing our relationship to her whole family just as they lost their brother.

Grace is dating Evan, the brother of the father of her child.

Their looks of shock couldn't compare to my devastation in that moment.

I'd never wished for a floor to open up and swallow me, but right then I had.

We hadn't killed Stefan, not that I've ever thought for a moment her insane ramblings were true. He'd been thirty years old for fuck's sake! Shock from finding out his brother was dating the mother of his child wouldn't have killed a perfectly healthy man.

And although we discovered Stefan died from an enlarged heart, it hadn't prevented Evan from pulling away from me.

I need him, but Yvette's cruel words really got into his head and I'm the one paying for it, as is my daughter.

So, in the past year, I've lost my best friend Elizabeth due to my own stupidity, Stefan in death, and Evan, too.

Not to mention Lyndsey, my daughter, turning four just weeks before her father died.

Never in a million years did I think I would have to explain why daddy wasn't around and why she would never see him again. What, as a mother, could I have said other than the truth? So I told her and we both cried our hearts out.

I never loved Stefan and we weren't really friends even after our drunken one night stand that resulted in my pregnancy, but he was my daughter's father. She needs him and now, all she has left of him is his family.

A family I know only keeps me around because I'm the mother of Stefan's daughter.

It hurts like a bitch and always has.

But the pain couldn't end there though, right?

Of course not. Nothing will ever be that simple in my life.

Stefan had been well off. He owned a business, Pierce & Pierce Enterprise, which was a profitable one that ended up expanding into three locations across the state.

Evan was his partner from the very beginning. Stefan had been the brains behind the software while Evan collaborated but also took care of the financial side of things.

It wasn't that Stefan hadn't been good with money; he just preferred to let somebody else take care of the paperwork.

This all started right after we slept together. He'd been a mess, but once he came out of his depression over Elizabeth leaving, he threw himself into starting a business and it blossomed.

Evan joined him.

Together, they both had a new purpose and left their old jobs behind for doing something they both loved. When Stefan died, I had no idea what would happen to his side of the business.

I should've known everything would've been taken care of from the onset.

Evan invited me to the office a few weeks after Stefan's death, only to tell me that when they started the business, an agreement had been drawn up. Something that would, in cases like these, make sure everything went smoothly.

Then, he told me that by law, Lyndsey is Stefan's heir and after her birth, the agreement had been updated with that information.

So technically, my daughter now owns half of quite a profitable company. Then, just as I inquired about what happened next, a man I'd only met a few times came into the room.

Geoffrey Lazarski, mutual friend of Evan and Stefan's, and in my opinion, a complete and utter bastard, took a seat next to Evan, making me feel nauseous.

"Grace," he'd said with a frown. "Sorry we're meeting under these circumstances."

"Thanks."

Evan laid some papers in front of me and began explaining what I'd see on them.

In essence, Evan and Geoffrey were named trustees. Stefan allowed for Geoffrey to buy out twenty-five percent of his stake upon his death, leaving Lyndsey with a twenty-five percent stake and the profits of any future sale and his estate, all monies to be put into a trust until she turned twenty-one. That is, all monies except for a yearly stipend given in monthly increments for the care and upbringing of his daughter.

When Evan named the amount, my mouth dropped open because my baby would be take care of for life.

They told me how it would all work and after I signed some papers, I went home when Evan and Geoffrey began to talk about something else.

No look, no hug, no anything from Evan. He pretended we were nothing and had never been anything. He had been cold, distant…unfailingly polite.

And even though I wanted to scream, I didn't at the time.

Months have passed since that day and still Evan barely acknowledges my existence.

The pain comes with the fact he's been overseeing my daughter's trust for a long time, which means I can't totally ignore him.

I ache and pine for the man I'd spent two years having a secret relationship with and love with all my heart.

But now, a whole year and a half has passed since Stefan died and I'm over it, the anger at Evan's abrupt desertion of me spilling over and erupting despite my efforts to keep it contained.

Today, he'll talk to me, one way or the other.

I DISCOVERED Evan's interest in me when Lyndsey was only eighteen months old.

Even after Stefan's family were told we were having a child together, we never really spent much time together. His sisters threw me a baby shower, planned along with my mother, but otherwise, nada. And truly, I hadn't minded. We weren't together, so it wasn't like I would become part of the family in the form of a wife.

Evan had been polite but distant at that point. However, he was a great uncle, always bringing Lyndsey presents and treats, often to my displeasure because she would want sweets instead of dinner. She adored him and the rest of the family, which was lucky because she was the only grandchild and many people loved her.

No mother could really ask for more.

Then, things changed.

Why or how, I don't really know. I didn't do anything different from what I always had, yet Evan began coming around more often.

At first, I thought it rather innocent. Even though Stefan was highly involved with Lyndsey, I've always been a single mother. I had my place along with a full-time job and sometimes I needed help, whether it involved something needing fixed or installed.

The first time Evan offered to help and told me he'd do it again if only I would just ask before he left. So I did ask, because I really had better things to do with my time than fix the pipes under my kitchen sink.

What was innocent? His offer, of course. But there wasn't anything innocent about my acceptance. He would come over dressed in a t-shirt and jeans, only to take off his t-shirt to work and wow, I would have to walk away to fan myself after a few moments. Nothing like a half naked man laying on your floor getting dirty for you.

Things escalated from there.

Offering him drinks afterward went from quickly handing him a glass of water to making sure our hands touched as often as possible. Every single time, honestly.

He would look at me with those sexy eyes of his and grin, showcasing his dimples before slowly drinking the water. Oh, he knew what he did to me and relished in it.

Before then, I'd never seen him smile much as he'd always been rather serious but around me, it was like he forgot to be that person. He would smile and tease me, and lift my daughter up to twirl her around, laughing like crazy as she giggled along.

One night just after Lyndsey turned two, Evan showed up at my door. I'd already put her to bed when he knocked.

"We need to talk," he said, the serious look back on his face. "Can I come in?"

I stepped back, instant anxiety making my stomach flip. What could he possibly want to talk about?

I didn't have to wonder long. No sooner was he inside the door and it shut than he had my back pressed up against it.

"Here's the problem, Grace," he stated flat out. "I like you."

Smiling, I tilted my head. "I like you, too. And so does Lyndsey."

He flirted with me before, but I never considered it as all that serious, and he seemed so angry right then at my response.

"No." He shook his head, a rueful grin on his face. "Not innocently, Grace. I…I really like you."

That's when he brought his body real close and rocked against me gently.

I felt every inch of him, and I do mean every inch.

"Oh." Really. That's all I could say. Yep. My mouth even hung open a little.

He didn't say anything, just stared at me with his serious face as I tried to figure out what to say.

When his eyes dropped to my mouth, the fight to deny our feelings for each other was over.

Yet he still fought it and honestly, I figured maybe we should. Dating the brother of the father of my child? Wouldn't that be strange?

"I don't know what to do…" He kept his hands on the door behind me as he struggled to find the right words. "I didn't expect to feel this way."

I hadn't said anything. Really, being naughty didn't seem that terrible of a thing in the moment. Evan was gorgeous and here he stood, all six feet and two hundred pounds of him with barely an inch of fat, telling me how much he wanted me. Nothing really would have stopped me, but I decided to mess with him anyway.

"What way? Sisterly?"

His eyes flicked down my body and back up, flaring as they met mine once again.

"I feel anything except brotherly towards you, Grace."

I placed one hand on his chest and the other on his shoulder, before sliding it up to rest on the back of his neck.

"You might kiss me and feel nothing."

"Or," he tossed back, raising an eyebrow. "I might kiss you and feel everything, baby."

If I were the swooning type, I might have then, but he hadn't given me the chance before capturing my lips with his.

There'd been no denying it then. He'd been right.

He kissed me and I let him feel everything.

And that was how our love affair began.

two

SINCE LYNDSEY TURNED FIVE EARLIER THIS YEAR, SHE'S IN kindergarten.

It had been hard to face Evan and his family for her birthday party, as she's a niece and a granddaughter to them while I'm merely her mother.

I wanted to scream at them, tell them if it wasn't for me, none of them would have Lyndsey at all, but I doubt they would have cared. They were polite to me because as her mother, I can tell them all to fuck off and there isn't a damn thing they can do.

And at the time, Evan continued to keep his distance and I kept mine, even as I cried on the inside.

I don't care about them, truly. I don't care about the money or the business or what Stefan left her. All I care about is, and always will be, the wellbeing of my little girl.

Making sure she grows up happy and healthy, knowing her father loved her, is all that matters.

She still cries for him occasionally and I'll always join right in because when my daughter is in pain, I am, too.

And now, she goes to class without an issue, happy to be there, while I stand at the entrance to the classroom, blubbering like a fool. She turns and waves at me, the smile on her face the first of its kind I've seen since her father died.

School's been good for her. She learns and has made new friends, all while giving her something else to think about than missing her dad.

With a final wave, I leave the school and drive the few minutes to my house.

I took the day off work today after a rather rough weekend. I don't know why I didn't just tell them I would be in a little late. Sitting around my house surely won't solve anything. And truly, I have nothing to do.

I've never had many friends in my entire life. Elizabeth and I became friends at college, but we last saw each other at Stefan's funeral. I don't count when I see her around town, because we never speak. She smiles at me from time to time, yet I never approach her, still ashamed at my behavior and how I wronged both her and Stefan.

I just can't do it, despite my desire to make things right between us.

Now, she's married to Simon and they have a baby. I've seen him in passing, as she carries him around in her arms. An adorable, chubby faced little guy with Simon's blond hair — I don't know how old he is now; nine or ten months, I guess.

That's what I want, by the way. Not that I don't love my

daughter, because I adore her with all I have. But I want more kids. Another baby, or maybe two or three. I'll have many as I can if I have the chance.

With Evan, of course.

I know what people will think, what they can't help but consider. After all, I've had a child with Stefan. To have a child with his brother? Some will say it's gross, but it isn't like that, not to me.

After all, me and Stefan hadn't *meant* to get together. We had a one night stand after Elizabeth left, when both of us felt as though our hearts out had been ripped out.

She'd been attacked on a night out with me, while Stefan had been out of the country and soon after, she became a different person. Stefan and I stupidly tried to find solace in each other after she kicked him to the curb and then disappeared without a word of goodbye.

He stepped up when I told him I became pregnant as result, but that had been all between us. We never dated, never even attempted; we were just two very different people who had a child and nothing else except an old, similar heartache.

Evan, though? At only eighteen months younger than Stefan, I've always thought him the more handsome of the two. Same dark blue eyes, but Evan inherited his father's hair color; a rich black hue, so dark there's a blueish sheen when wet or in the light.

Where Stefan had been a hot head, Evan is level headed and austere. He takes his work serious and doesn't put up with crap from anybody. I've always admired that, as he's strong where I lack. He stays calm even when upset, while I tend avoid conflict at all costs. He's the sunshine when I feel as if I'm drowning in the rain. We are two halves of a whole. At least, I thought we were.

Angry at him all over again, I look down at my phone to see the time.

11 a.m.

By the time I get to his work, he'll be on lunch. He always eats lunch in his office because he says it's the only time he gets to himself.

Well, not today. Today, I'll get my answer, even if I have to get naked to make him talk to me.

Before I truly think through my plan, and the potential consequences, I head out to give him a piece of my mind.

***

"Is he in?"

His secretary, I dunno her name nor do I care to know what it is, just stares at me, scowling.

"Yes, he is, but you can't just barge in."

"Sure I can." I smile brightly at her. "Don't announce me, unless you'd like me to tell him you're out here texting."

Her eyes widen as I storm past her desk. She probably wonders how I know, which is really simple—I watched her while approaching her desk. Texting is actually forbidden and if she gets caught, she'll be fired.

She's mute as I turn the handle of his office door and step inside, closing it gently behind me.

"Alexis, you're supposed to knock—"

Evan turns in his chair, his words cutting off at the sight of me.

Alexis. So that's her name. I file that information away for use later, if necessary.

"Hello, Evan."

He stares at me, his face closing up. His eyes don't burn brightly like they used to and my chest tightens, stomach roiling.

What am I doing? He's made it clear he doesn't want me, so why did I show up like this? Why do I torture myself?

Oh right, I want to hear him say it, so I'm going to be as outrageous as possible. Maybe I've been too nice. Hell, no maybe about it. I let him thrust me aside without saying a word, but no more.

"You know, considering you fucked me for two years, the least you can do is say hi."

"Don't be crude, Grace. It doesn't become you."

I laugh, mocking his words. "It doesn't *become* me?" He's always loved using what I consider proper and uptight speech. "You know what doesn't become you? Treating me like I'm a slut you got sick of and just tossed aside without so much as a 'thanks for the fun.'"

He flinches then, but doesn't get up. He continues to pick at his food, now refusing to look at me.

I stomp closer, my heels digging into the plush carpet of the room. "Talk to me, damn you."

Nothing.

I slap my hand on the desk upon reaching it, making him jump at the sudden violent action from me.

"Admit it. All a game to you, huh? Did you enjoy it? Did you enjoy treating me like a fuck toy only to decide I wasn't worth it once your brother died?"

I'm not making any sense, and I know it, but want nothing more than to piss him off.

His face goes pale at the mention of Stefan, his mouth pinching with anger. Yet, he still doesn't speak.

"Two years I let you hide me like something to be ashamed of, when I never gave two fucks what he thought. You said you would tell him, but you were full of fucking shit! You were never going to tell him. How long were you gonna lie to me, to yourself?"

My voice raises, near to yelling as he finally reacts.

His eyes burn now as he stands up and slaps his own hands on the surface of his desk, leaning forward until our faces are inches apart.

"Get out," he says through clenched teeth.

I can almost taste his anger, his voice seething and want to crow with victory.

"Or what?"

Oh, I'll taunt him. He isn't a man you want to do that to, but I'm beyond caring. I'm hurt and between the two of us, he's done the most hurting.

He doesn't answer. Fine, I'm more than willing to play this game.

I step away and he relaxes a little.

Then, walking back to the door, I glance over my

shoulder while turning the lock.

"What are you doing?"

He doesn't bellow. Oh no, that's not dignified. The question is low and threatening, however.

I don't respond, merely turning around with a dazzling smile on my face. I kick off one heel, then the other, not caring where they land. Stalking closer to him, I slowly unbutton my blouse, watching his face the entire time.

Evan doesn't move, even as I walk around his desk and stand at his side.

I let my blouse slide down and fall to the floor, leaving me in my black satin bra and layered black skirt. Reaching up, I tug my hair free of its messy bun, the hair falling around my shoulders and down my back with ease, where it touches the very top of my ass.

He's always loved to grab onto it and he isn't unaffected now. He's gripping the desk with both hands, his knuckles white even though he still hasn't faced me, although he's watching me out of the corner of his eyes.

"Put your clothes on, Grace," he commands, his jaw tight. "My office is not an appropriate—"

"When *is* it appropriate to speak to you, or to fuck you Evan?" I cut him off, tugging my skirt down until I can kick it off. "On your timeline? Well, screw you. I'm sick of your way and now, now we're going to do it my way."

His body practically quivers with the effort it takes not to touch me. I know him. Two long years together means I can read his body like a book and he wants me. Now I just have to get him to touch me, because it will all be over then. I'll have to touch him first, though, because stubborn is his middle name apparently.

Taking off my bra, I drop it to the floor, clad now only in my lacy black panties—his fave. Then, I step behind him and place my hands on his back.

He removed his suit jacket for lunch and wears only his white button up dress shirt. Up and down, I stroke his back, before sliding my hands around the side and to his front, hugging him as I simply breathe him in. My cheek against his back, I hear and feel his shuddering breath, which makes me smile happily.

"It's been a long year, Evan," I say softly. "A very long and lonely year. I want you."

He straightens then and I slide around to the front of his body, my own barely fitting between him and the desk. I start undoing his belt, feeling his hot gaze on me yet not looking up at him. I don't acknowledge him as I pull the belt free and toss it to the side. Unbuttoning his pants, I lick my lips in anticipation.

Then, he groans, and I want to cheer as he brings a hand up to wrap in my hair, gripping it tightly. But I don't feel the pain, only the pleasure of having him touch me after so long.

Tugging my hair, my head falls back as I stare up into his eyes. His mouth descends on mine, instantly seeking access to my mouth with a punishing thrust of his tongue. I moan, his grip tightening as his other arm reaches around and moves something, most likely his lunch. His desk is usually oddly clean, everything kept in a certain spot and always put away for lunch. I'm certainly not complaining.

He pulls away, murmuring, "Lean over the desk, now."

Excitement courses through me, not even caring that he's turned into the boss. I'm going to get what I came for and that's all that matters right this moment.

As I turn and do as bid, he releases my hair only to grip my hips and push against me. I wiggle my bottom and he groans, his hands shuffling around for a few moments. Then, he slips my panties down and exposes me to the air, before slipping his hand between my legs.

His touch light, I move against his hand, trying to extract every bit of enjoyment I can out of this.

The quick replacement of his hand with his arousal makes me gasp. His grip on my hips tightens as he slowly enters me from behind, torturing me with the slow pace. With nothing to grab onto, I first my hands and bring one up to my mouth to stifle any noises. At the same time, one of his hands releases my hip and slips beneath me, stroking where our bodies are connected even as the pressure of his hand keeps our bodies flush against one another. His other hand curls in my hair again, bringing my head back enough to bare my neck as he leans over my body.

"Is this what you wanted?" Smooth and creamy, that's how his question comes out. Calm and collected, because he hasn't lost his cool, he's merely taken control of the situation. "You win, Grace. I hope you're proud of yourself."

With that he pulls away only to slam back in, my head motionless within his grasp. My breasts just barely touch the top of the desk in this position, yet my nipples tighten at the glancing rub on the surface.

I want to scream, "Yes! Yes, I am very proud!" but I can't think anymore. Hell, I don't even want to breathe.

All I can do is feel everything as the man I adore possesses me on his desk. We've never done this before, we wouldn't have dared and I've been here lots before with one excuse or another. It is forbidden and sweet, as I'm now fully naked and he, still clothed. His clothing touches me as he moves and it only increases the naughtiness in my mind.

In, out. I match my breathing pace with his as he touches me at the same time, soft caresses that seem at odds with the ferocity of his movements. His body over mine, he releases his grip on my hair and pushes it to one side, kissing my neck and shoulders as he keeps up the punishing pace. I know he's close as his breathing increases and thanks to the manipulation of his hand, I'm not far behind.

As my body lets go, so does his. I stiffen as my orgasm rips through me, the hand against my mouth doing its job in muting me. He, on the other hand, isn't prepared and lets out a loud moan of his own. And while he holds onto me as if he's holding on for dear life, his mouth hovers near my ear.

"Better than my imagination," he murmurs.

The amusement in his voice catches me by surprise and I laugh. He releases my hair and steps back, straightening his clothing.

Mourning the closeness already, I turn around and use my arms to support me against the desk as I watch him.

"Get dressed, please." The command is soft, matching the expression on his face.

I slide my panties back up and walk away to pick up my skirt. Slipping it on, I don't look at him even at the sound of him buckling his belt.

He doesn't say anything else and soon, we're both dressed as if nothing happened. Except my hair, which I don't put back up in a bun, and he stares at before clearing his throat.

"I have to get back to work."

Clipped and back to business, as he sits in his chair and attends to his tie.

Already irritated at his tone, my hands ball into fists. "I better see you later."

This isn't a request, but a demand, and his eyes fly to mine in complete acknowledgment as he states, "Oh, you can count on it, Grace, especially after this little spectacle of yours."

He glances at me from head to toe before focusing on his computer screen, summarily dismissing me.

I should be pissed at his attitude after what we've just done. Yet, I'm not, because he gave me exactly what I wanted and for the moment, I'm happy.

Even if I know he's going to make me pay for it oh so sweetly later.

"Bye bye, darling," I say in a super sweet voice, throwing a kiss in his direction upon opening the door.

And as it closes behind me, I swear the sound of his laughter follows me down the hall.

three

A FEW DAYS HAVE PASSED SINCE MY VISIT TO HIS OFFICE BUT I'm certain Evan will come see me sooner rather than later.

Exhausted from work and the adjustment of both me and Lyndsey to her new school schedule, a hot shower followed by a relaxing drink are in order.

It's Friday night, she's sound asleep and I have the next two days off. Tonight will be all about me and then this weekend, we will go do something fun together, just the two of us.

As I walk upstairs, my phone dings with a text from Evan, and my heart speeds up at the message he's sent.

Up for company?

That's all it says and I want to cheer.

Instead, I send a quick reply before rushing to get ready since I don't know how far away he is.

> Absolutely. I'm hopping in the shower, see you soon!

I jump when the door opens a few minutes later as I'm rinsing out my hair. Seeing his frame through the blurry sliding doors, I sigh with relief, and can't deny I'm glad he wasn't as far away as I thought. "Fuck Evan, you scared me!"

He laughs, the sound rusty and unused. "You knew I was coming. Besides who else has a key?"

Okay, he has a point.

"Right. I'll be out soon."

"No need," he replies. I can see him taking his shirt off through the glass and swallow hard as he adds, "I'm joining you."

I want to dance with happiness as Evan steps inside the shower and shuts the door, giving me a brief opportunity to drink him in.

He looks good. No, better than that, he looks fantastic, as if he's been working out even more than usual. His body — which is pretty damn rock solid — puts mine to shame and I exercise as much as I can.

I ache to reach out and touch him, but I don't. I lift my gaze back up to his, only to find him perusing my form from under heavy-lidded eyes.

When he finally speaks, the desire in his voice is thick and makes me shiver in anticipation. "Are you done washing your hair?"

At my nod, his mouth curves in the way he has, displaying his very lickable dimples, as he takes a step closer to me. I automatically step back and his smile grows wider. Picking up the soap from the side of the shower, he motions for me to turn around with his other hand.

Only a few seconds pass with him washing my back before I ask him what I've been wanting to know for a while now. "What happened, Evan?"

He doesn't even pause as he sighs before saying, "I don't have a good answer. I wasn't sure I could do this anymore."

I whirl around—well, as fast as one can in a shower without falling flat on their ass—and glare at him. "Don't you think you could have, oh I don't know, said something to me maybe?"

"I'm here now, aren't I?" He brings a hand up to my shoulder and I smack it away. "Ow! What the hell?"

"Yeah, you're here now," I snap, any good feelings toward him gone as if they were never there in the face of his cowardice. "Where have you been for a year, besides ignoring me and my daughter? Your niece, I might add, who got pretty damned used to you being around. It's not bad enough she lost her father, but you just go pull your little fucking stunt and hurt her even more!"

He doesn't reply, the only display of emotion in the grim set of his mouth. But he hadn't looked away during my rant, which strangely pleases me. Like he knows he deserves it. Good, because he does.

"And me. You hurt me." Tears fill my eyes, but I'm beyond caring. This is my chance to get out my feelings and I take it. "You're in my shower, but only, *only*, because I stormed into your office the other day. I took the risk, not you. I always take the risks and you always play it safe and it is such bullshit, Evan. Complete and utter bullshit and you know it!"

He must notice the water getting cooler because he reaches around and turns it up enough to make sure the temp is how I prefer it before placing his hands on my shoulders.

"I'm sorry, Grace."

"Are you?" I love him with all my heart, yet the disappearing act he pulled makes it so difficult to believe him. "I wish I could be sure you mean it."

"This hasn't been easy for me, either." His jaw tightens, hands slipping from my shoulders before he shoves one through his hair while the other drops to hang at his side. "Stefan's death was unexpected and you know how close we were."

"I shared a child with him."

"We shared an entire *life* and business," he retorts while stepping back, the wall between us once more, although I'm not sure why because my statement was meant to tell him I understand. "He was my brother as well as my best friend and…"

"And what?"

His face colors, as I've never seen it do before, as he softly admits, "And he knew about us the whole time, Grace."

Those words are the last thing I expect to hear him say, my heart jumping into my throat. "What?"

"The day after that night when I told you how I felt, my guilt over it drove me to tell him, because we never hid anything from one another." When my mouth drops open, his own lips twist as he glances away, and then grabs the shower curtain tightly in his fist. "I asked him not to tell you he knew, because I wanted to tell you when I was sure about our relationship."

I swear, my heart's breaking into a million pieces at his admission, because we were together for *two years*, and my voice breaks as I whisper, "When you were sure?"

"Yes."

That's all he says, after *two* fucking years of what I thought was sneaking around.

Unbelievable.

As the ache in my chest grows to an almost unbearable degree, I turn toward the shower knob and turn it off, not caring I haven't finished with everything as I face him again. "You need to go."

"Grace—"

"God, Evan, just get the fuck out."

He keeps his gaze locked on mine and the most difficult thing to do is not to reach out to him. I haven't felt as alive as the other day in his office in a long time, but this man isn't behaving like the one I fell in love with, not by a long shot.

If after two years, he hadn't been sure about us, would he ever have been? What if Stefan hadn't died? How long would the deception have gone on, with me feeling a little guilty over keeping us a secret from his family the whole time?

"No, I won't," he finally says into the silence between us.

"I'm here now, Grace, and it isn't because you stormed into my office the other day."

"Too fucking bad for you, Evan." Grabbing the door, I slide it open with a hard jerk and step out of the shower before he can stop me. "I wouldn't have bothered if I had known you weren't sure about us after two damn years of sneaking around."

"Who says I wasn't?"

"I don't care."

And maybe I should. Maybe I'm being too rash, refusing to listen to anything he has to say on the matter, but right now, the wound he's opened in me is fresh and bleeding. I'm not willing to hear him tell me all the things I wish he would've told me before Stefan died, not willing to forgive him for his deception.

Not tonight.

"Get out," I say while slipping into my robe and tying to sash around my waist. "And lock the door behind you."

Then, I storm out of the bathroom, hoping he doesn't come after me because I don't think I can bear to say the words once more if he dares to touch me.

And when I'm in the safety of my room, the front door shutting after a few minutes, the tears I held back in the bathroom spring forth to stream down my cheeks until I'm too tired to keep my eyes open any longer.

four

Evan doesn't try to contact me in the weeks that follow his visit to my house.

I am a little disappointed, honestly, but that's my own doing. I've always thought he would fight for me, yet he never had, and this time doesn't seem any different so far.

Of course, the fact Stefan knew all along doesn't change things, except he obviously never had a problem with Evan and I being together, right?

Surely he would've said something if he had, a fact that makes me sad all over again with him not being here, because I could really use a talk with him right about now.

But, there's no one for me to talk to about this, and before I know it, Christmas has arrived.

Ever since I gave birth to Lyndsey, we've spent Christmas Eve with my mother, and Christmas morning with the entire Pierce family. Well, until the year before last, when my mother retired and moved somewhere far warmer. We saw her briefly last year, but she's never been really involved, as the whole situation with Stefan was something she disapproved of.

So, our holidays are now just spent with the Pierce's and this year the celebration is at Penny's. While I'm dreading the whole ordeal, Lyndsey is super excited to see everyone. Since beginning school, she sees them all a lot less than before, and so she can barely sit still on the drive to Penny's house.

I'm glad she'll have a good time, even though I'm not looking forward to sitting in a room with them all, feeling like I always do — as if I'm the one who doesn't belong.

And as we pull into the driveway, finding a parking space is a challenge since it appears almost everyone is here. I manage to find one after a few moments while noting, a little against my will and almost reflexively, that Evan isn't here yet.

An observation quickly rectified by his arrival as I help Lyndsey out of her car seat. She takes off running toward him with a squeal of happiness while I shut the car door and try hard to keep the smile on my face while approaching him. My daughter's arms and legs are wrapped tight around his neck and waist as he embraces her back, a wonderful sight considering he hasn't been around in a while.

But unlike adults, children forgive so easily, and to her, he's Evan, her most favorite uncle.

This whole moment makes me want to smack him, hard, for what he's put us both through; apparently, for nothing, since Stefan knew all along.

When Lyndsey wiggles to let him know she wants him to put her down, he obliges, and she grabs my free hand with a toothy grin. "Can we go inside now, Mommy?"

"Of course."

Evan's car door opens and shuts as we head toward the front door, but by the time Penny answers the door, Evan's standing behind both of us on the porch with an armful of presents.

The door opens, Penny smiling at us. "Why are you standing out here in the cold? Come on in!" She steps back with an inviting wave and grins down at Lyndsey. "I'm so happy to see you, sweetheart!"

Lyndsey runs past her with a breathless, "Hi, Aunty Penny!"

Penny laughs as I slip out of my shoes and she hugs me before greeting Evan over my shoulder. "You're late!"

"I had a lot of presents to wrap." At that, I feel him tug at the gift in my hand and say, "I'll take this in for you."

No point in arguing, I suppose.

Penny releases me, her smile empathetic as if she completely understands what's going on, and then leads the way toward the living room, where Lyndsey is waiting for us. When we follow her into the room, I'm aware of everyone's eyes on us, and we sit in the chairs Penny points us toward.

Evan sits down beside me. Not because I want him to, but it seems these are the only three open seats, and they're all close to me.

Terrific.

To avoid looking at him, I glance around the room, and

my eyes land on Yvette. She's facing my direction and when her gaze meets mine, a nervous smile finds it way to my lips for no reason at all.

She nods at me, her eyes flicking away from mine to my daughter's when Lyndsey squeals, "Aunty Vet! I missed you!"

I watch as she opens her arms and Lyndsey runs right into them, embracing my little girl as she declares just as loudly, "Lyndsey! I missed you more!"

Lyndsey draws back with her little toothy smile and shakes her head, sending her pigtails swinging as she gives what seems is her favorite phrase for months now. "Nuh-uh. I missed you more to infinity!"

Yvette exaggerates her response, her body going back against the couch as she covers her eyes with one arm and sends Lyndsey into a fit of giggles. "Oh no, you win! Where did you learn to say that? I can't possibly beat you now!"

"You're silly, Aunty Vet!" Lyndsey pulls on Yvette's arm. "I brought you a present! I helped mommy wrap it, but she said it will make you really happy because I chose it."

"Yeah?"

Yvette glances this way and my face warms, something about the look in her eye making me uncomfortable. I manage to smile at her, but then Evan distracts me before I can examine the emotion any further.

"I'm sorry, Grace."

Sure he is. "So you've said."

"My apology isn't enough for you? What do you want me to say?"

"Nothing now," I hiss at him, because this isn't the place

for us to have this conversation. "You should've said a whole lot, a long time ago. That's what I think."

"God, you're impossible."

His comment nearly makes me forget where we are, but luckily Lyndsey suddenly catches my attention as she yells across the room. "Mommy! I want to give Aunty Vet her present right now! Can I, can I?"

Right now, I'm glad for her presence, as she distracts me from saying something I shouldn't to Evan and forces me to relax enough to smile her way. "Of course you may, honey. It's your present, she can have it whenever you want."

Lyndsey claps, turns back to Yvette real quick, then runs over to the tree to go through the presents. I watch her take it back over to Yvette, who unwraps it slowly, and my eyes mist when she catches sight of what she now holds in her hands.

My daughter says something, probably explaining where we found the picture of Yvette and Stefan, and I take that opportunity to take a deep breath in an effort to calm my emotions before they run out of control.

As I wipe a tear off my face, I glance back over at Lyndsey and Yvette, who thanks me with a silent movement of her mouth, and it's enough to bring a smile to my own lips. She's never thanked me for anything and although her little spectacle at the hospital threw the whole situation with Evan into the rest of family's storm, that picture belongs in her possession.

"Are you all right?"

Evan's question is soft and concerned, just for my ears,

and I turn to him, shrugging, playing off the emotions as if they're no big deal. "Lyndsey is just such a sweetheart."

"She takes after her mother."

If we were together, if he hadn't kept something important from me and spent the last year and a half ignoring me… I might believe he sees me that way.

But I can't.

Today, I'm not ready to trust another word he says to me, no matter how hard my heart beats or my body aches for him to touch me just one more time.

So I focus on the festivities, trying my best to push the heartache aside until I'm alone again later.

I'M in Penny's kitchen washing some dishes to get away from the crazy level of noise in the living room when I hear Elizabeth's voice from the doorway softly say, "Oh, hey Grace."

Surprised she's talking to me, I glance over my shoulder with a quick smile, only to stop at the sight of her son in her arms. He's focused on his mother's face, while Elizabeth waits for me to respond.

I turn off the water, grab a towel and dry my hands while returning her greeting. "Hi. Merry Christmas."

"Yes, it is," she replied with a laugh, lifting Sam into the air and smiling up at him while he giggles. "How have you been?"

I'm not sure what to think. It's been silence from so many

angles since Stefan died and the fact she's asking me anything is a little confusing. I shrug because what else can I do? I don't know what we are anymore, because neither of us were very good friends to the other when it mattered most. "Okay. How about you?"

"Good." She lowers Sam and cradles him in her arms while walking across the room, then holds him out to me, smiling. "Will you hold him while I make him a bottle? He's a little hungry kiddo today."

"Sure." Sam gurgles happily, staring up at me with wide eyes while reaching for his cute bootie covered feet. It's impossible not to grin at him, this being the first time I've been this close to him, and as my heart squeezes I whisper, "Hi, you."

And there it is… the ache I try to ignore and have for years. The one where I want nothing more than to have another baby, which seems less and less in the cards for me as time has passed.

Elizabeth must notice something in my expression because her voice gentles. "He likes you already. Look at that smile."

Sam does seem content, making soft baby sounds while I rock him slightly. The kitchen feels suddenly too quiet, filled with unspoken things between Elizabeth and me.

"Grace," she starts, then stops, seeming to struggle with her words. "I know things have been... complicated between us. Especially after everything that happened."

I shift Sam in my arms, not quite meeting her eyes. "That's one way to put it."

"I wanted to say I'm sorry. For the way things were with Stefan before he died. I had no right to interfere, especially knowing about you and Evan." She pauses. "Though I have to admit, I'm still not entirely sure what's going on there."

The directness catches me off guard. I glance toward the doorway to make sure we're alone, then look back at her. "Join the club. I'm not sure either anymore."

"But you love him."

It's not a question, and I don't deny it. "Loving someone and being with them are two different things, aren't they? You should know that better than anyone."

She flinches slightly, and I immediately regret the sharpness in my tone. "I'm sorry. That was..."

"True," she finishes quietly. "And deserved." She pulls formula and a bottle from the diaper bag. "For what it's worth, I can see the way he looks at you. Even today. Especially today."

"What do you mean?"

"He's watches you constantly, Grace. Every time you move, his eyes follow. And when that cousin of Richard's was talking to you earlier? I thought Evan might actually get up and come over."

I think about the older man who'd cornered me by the Christmas tree, asking overly personal questions about my "situation" and whether I planned to find Lyndsey a "proper father figure." Evan had been across the room talking to Simon, but now that she mentions it...

"He didn't though," I point out.

"No, but he looked like he wanted to." She tests the

bottle temperature on her wrist. "The old Evan would have stayed in his seat and pretended not to notice. This one looked ready to start a fight."

Sam begins to fuss, and I hand him back to her, watching as she settles him with the bottle. The sight tugs at something deep in my chest because of the easy competence of motherhood and the way Sam immediately calms in her arms.

"Can I ask you something?" When she nods, I softly continue, "When you and Stefan were... whatever you were... how did you know when it was worth fighting for versus when it was time to let go?"

She's quiet for a long moment, focused on Sam. Finally, she looks up. "I think you fight until you can't anymore. Until you've given everything you have and there's nothing left. But the key is making sure the other person is fighting too." She pauses. "I spent too much time fighting for someone who wasn't doing their part until it was too late. Don't make my mistake, Grace. Don't be the only one fighting."

Before I can respond, Lyndsey bursts through the kitchen doorway. "Mommy! Uncle Evan said he'd push me on the swing if you said okay!"

I glance out the window at the old swing set in Penny's backyard, then back at my daughter's eager face. "It's pretty cold out there, sweetheart."

"I'll wear my coat! Please? He asked if I wanted to and I said yes but then he said I had to ask you first!"

Elizabeth smiles. "Looks like Uncle Evan is being responsible. Maybe some fresh air would be good."

I nod, trying to ignore the flutter in my stomach at the thought of Evan doing something so normal, so... fatherly. "Alright, but bundle up tight."

As Lyndsey races off to get her coat, Elizabeth touches my arm. "Grace? For what it's worth, I hope you figure it out. Both of you deserve to be happy."

"Thanks," I manage, surprised by how much her words mean to me.

Not even two minutes later through the window, I watch Evan emerge into the backyard with Lyndsey, already pushing his sleeves up despite the cold. He's crouched down to her level, helping her onto the swing, and she's chattering away at him with the endless energy of a five-year-old. He looks relaxed in a way I haven't seen in months, and for just a moment, I let myself imagine what it would be like if this was our normal—family gatherings, him being present not just physically but emotionally.

But then I remember Elizabeth's words about fighting alone, and I force myself to look away.

five

I BLINK AT THE RANDOM TEXT FROM EVAN.

Of course I haven't gone out, even though it's New Year's Eve. Lyndsey's in bed, midnight is approaching fast, and I've been enjoying a peaceful evening at home with a couple glasses of wine.

Similar to how I've spent every night this week, actually, as going out isn't something I've done much of since getting pregnant with Lyndsey.

I became a mother and parenting her is something I've put first above all else ever since the day she was born.

And that's why I have to admit this whole mess with Evan isn't all his fault despite my acting as if it is. I've spent the last few days thinking about what he said, including remembering all the time we spent together, and the truth is, I'm as responsible as he is.

A little part of me enjoyed the secrecy of our relationship, of the nights he came over late, only to leave early in the morning before anyone knew he was there.

Despite me not wanting to tell Stefan, unsure of what his reaction might be, there hadn't been anything stopping me from saying something no matter what Evan desired.

Nope, I'm not innocent. Lyndsey was Stefan's daughter, Evan his brother, and I spent every moment after our first kiss worrying what his family would think of us dating.

Stupid.

We were two grown adults and had no reason to feel ashamed of how we felt about one another. Not like any of them cared when they did find out. Well, outside of Yvette, who is never happy with anything anyway.

Should he have said something about Stefan knowing? Absolutely. Does the fact he didn't fall all on him? No, because I could've told Stefan, and if I had, he might have told me he knew about my relationship with Evan, that he was okay with it.

So, what the hell am I doing, staring down at his text and wondering if I should answer or not?

Maybe letting him go is the best course of action, but when it comes to Evan, when have I ever done what is best?

Never. I'm not really one to take the easiest way out. Well, okay, not much at all when compared to years ago.

I finally answer him, hoping I'm not making a big mistake.

No, I'm at home. Why?

His reply is fast, succinct, and reflective of my own feelings.

Because I want to see you.

Nice. I smile because he doesn't ask. He tells me what he wants and leaves the rest up to me. Not typical behavior from him, which perhaps finally demonstrates his understanding of how pissed off I've been.

Do you? How far away are you?

Close enough to be at your door in less than five minutes.

I bet if I say yes, he'll be here in less than two because chances are he's about to drive past my house. This is something he did before and if there's one thing Evan doesn't do, changing is it.

And knowing that, despite all he's put me through, I can't get him out of my heart or my head.

Tonight, even if it is *only* for tonight, I want him here with me and in my bed, because if nothing else, tomorrow is a new year, where I can start over if necessary.

Okay.

I send the simple message, then bite my lip between my teeth, hoping I'm not making a big mistake I'll regret come morning before sending another.

See you soon.

And my guess about his arrival ends up being correct.

He knocks at my door less than a few minutes after my final text and when I open the door, he strides in with a devious smile upon his lips.

Careful not to slam the door, he silently shrugs out of his coat and hangs it on the nearby hook, then hauls me into his warm embrace with a hushed, "Hey."

As my arms find their way around his neck, my reply just as quiet. "Hi."

"Thanks for letting me come over." Tipping his head, he kisses the side of my neck and up to my ear to whisper, "How about leading the way to your room?"

I know what we really need to do is talk, but I'm impatient to get close to him as always and it seems he's feeling the same way.

Perhaps the words we both need to say can wait until later. After all, what's another few hours going to hurt after the last year and a half of nothing?

Leading the way up the steps, we make it to my bedroom, and when darkness engulfs the both of us, we're each divested of our clothing by the other without a word.

"I've missed you," he murmurs, every step forward sending me back toward the bed, until my knees hit the edge. "And this."

Sitting down, I lift one hand and wrap my fingers around his hot, hard arousal with an unconscious lick to wet my lips in pure anticipation of the pleasure to come tonight.

With a brief smirk at the unintended pun, I enjoy the way he sucks in a breath when I lean in, running my tongue around the tip of him.

Even better when his hands spear into my hair, then grip it, holding my head immobile as my mouth opens wider to take more of him in.

We're good together like this, always have been despite all our other differences.

He moans with each thrust, my tongue swirling around his length, and before long, he's pushing me onto my back against the comforter.

My turn to shove my hands in his hair as he spreads my legs and crouches between them, head dipping down as he uses two fingers to expose me to his always hungry gaze.

Then, he takes care of me with his mouth and hands, something he's always done best, until I'm softly begging him for the sweet release I know he'll give me.

I'm blissfully floating when he lifts my legs straight and steps closer, entering my body slow and steady, torturing each of us by taking his time.

This is nothing like that day in his office. His lips devour mine as his hips rock, my mouth swallowing his moans and mine with each thrust. I can't think, my mind blank as he rips his mouth away and bites me gently on the shoulder as his body tightens, coming with one final thrust and a deep, satisfied groan.

Now that we've both got what we wanted, he rolls off me and stalks to the in-suite bathroom, returning with something to wash me with. Once finished, he tosses it next to the nearby laundry basket and climbs back onto the bed.

Once we've moved to the center of it, I cuddle close to his side with my head on his chest, and he kisses my forehead.

All this is done silently, something I'm glad for since I'm not really in the mood to talk, fearing the conversation we need to have will ruin the moment.

An opinion he must share as he simply says, "Happy New Year, Grace," his hand resting on the small of my back lightly caressing my bare skin as his breathing slowly returns to its normal, slow pace.

The familiar, comforting beat soon lulls me into one of the soundest sleep I've had since that day at his office, and morning arrives long before I'm ready for it with a loud bang from downstairs.

EVAN'S IN THE KITCHEN, doing something with one of the cupboard doors when I rush downstairs to see what all the racket is about.

Lyndsey stands a couple feet away from him, watching him work with rapt attention, and neither of them are aware of my arrival as I stand in the entryway.

Instead of announcing my presence, I join in on watching Evan doing what he does best, being handy around the house. I've been meaning to get that cupboard door fixed for ages, so if he wants to do it, then I'm going to let him have at it to save me time and money.

Before long, he's showing Lyndsey the door works now *and* no longer squeaks while she claps as if he's hung the moon for her.

That's when I laugh, startling them both, and Evan grins as Lyndsey runs over to hug me.

"Morning, Mommy! Uncle Evan fixed it!"

"I see that. And what do we say to him?"

"We say thank you!" She glances at over her shoulder and practically shouts, "Thank you!"

Then, she runs out of the kitchen, leaving me and Evan alone.

"Yes, thank you," I say as he walks toward me, a decidedly naughty gleam in his eyes. "I was going to get around to it."

"Now you don't need to worry." He stops a few inches in front of me and reaches out, circling his arms around my waist and drawing me closer until there's nothing left to do except place my hands on his shoulders. "Better. Good morning, baby."

Seems like we're going to continue to ignore what's happened before last night and since I'm not in the mood for an argument, I return his greeting with a smile. "Morning. I'm surprised you didn't leave before I got up."

"I'm not an asshole today." He chuckles when I roll my eyes and lowers his head to press a soft, sweet kiss on my mouth. "Did you get enough rest?"

"Yes, thank you. Better than in a while."

"Seemed like you needed to sleep in, so I kept Lyndsey occupied. She may be able to fix the cupboard next time," he jokes, releasing me after another quick kiss. "You two have plans for today?"

Walking over to the coffee maker, I grab a mug from the nearby cupboard and shrug. "Not really. You?"

"I'm all yours. Whatever you want to do. Any ideas?"

Lyndsey runs back into the kitchen, squealing as she latches onto Evan's arm and giggles. "I want to go skating! Can we go skating?"

"Ice skating?" Evan laughs at her exuberant nod and catches my eye even as he continues addressing her. "And what about your mom? Do you think she wants to go ice skating, too?"

She releases her hold on his leg, lifts her arms into the air while jumping up and down. "Yeah! She does! You want to go, right Mommy?"

Sipping at the hot coffee, I pucker my lips, pretending to consider it a lot before smiling at Lyndsey. "Of course. I love skating."

"Yay! Does that mean I can wear my special boots?"

"Yes, sweetheart, go ahead and get ready. We'll leave in a little bit, after I've had my coffee, all right?"

"Okay!"

We both watch her skip out of the room, where she'll go get dressed and play until we're ready to go as she's done in the past, and then Evan speaks to me again. "I love how happy she is. Always have."

"Me, too."

"She takes after you, Grace. You're one of the happiest people I know."

"You're sweet."

"I mean it."

I take a seat at the table with my coffee and release a heavy sigh. "Boy, you're really bringing your A-game this morning, Evan."

He pauses, the easy smile fading from his face. "What do you mean by that?"

I take another sip of coffee, studying him over the rim of my mug. "The charm offensive. Fixing things around the house, being great with Lyndsey, telling me I'm happy and sweet." I set the mug down carefully. "It's very... you."

"I'm not sure I follow." But there's something in his eyes that suggests he knows exactly what I mean.

"This is what you always do, Evan. You show up, you're perfect for a few hours or a day or three, you make me remember why I fell in love with you in the first place." I lean back in my chair. "And then what happens?"

He's quiet for a long moment, and I can see him choosing his words carefully. "Grace, last night—"

"Last night was wonderful," I interrupt. "Just like the office was wonderful. Just like all our stolen moments over the past few years were wonderful. But wonderful moments don't make a relationship."

"What are you saying?"

I stand up, needing some distance. "I'm saying I need more than your A-game, Evan. I need to know what happens tomorrow. And next week. And the next time something gets difficult or complicated or requires you to actually commit to something."

He follows me to the counter, yet doesn't touch me this time. "I'm here, aren't I?"

"You're here today. On New Year's Day. When it's easy and sweet and Lyndsey's excited about ice skating." I turn to face him. "Where were you when she had the flu and I was up all night with her? Where are you when she cries for her daddy at bedtime and I can't do anything except hold her?"

"Grace—"

"Where have you been for the past eighteen months, Evan?" My voice is steady, but I can feel the emotion building. "Not here. Not like me, here every single day taking care of my daughter and wondering if you are ever going to fight for us. Or wondering if you expect me to wait forever for you to decide we are worth the risk."

He runs a hand through his hair, and I recognize the gesture. He always does that when he's cornered and looking for an escape route.

"Don't," I say quietly before he can make up some bullshit to try and leave. "Don't you dare shut down on me now. Not after last night. Not after you waltzed in here this morning fixing things and acting like we're a family."

His gaze softens, his body relaxing a little. "We could be."

"Could be isn't good enough anymore." I cross my arms. "I love you, Evan. I've loved you for years now. But I won't keep being the only one taking all the risks while you play it safe and keep one foot out the door."

His jaw tightens. "That's not fair."

"Isn't it? Tell me one time, just one, where you've put yourself on the line for us. Where you've been the one to make the first move, take the leap, fight for what we have."

The silence stretches between us, and I can hear Lyndsey upstairs, singing to herself as she gets ready.

"I thought so," I whisper.

There's no solutions here, because his silence says more than anything else, and the fact he doesn't tell me he loves me back only confirms what I already know deep down.

I'm the only one fighting.

"I should get ready," I say finally, my voice surprisingly calm. "Lyndsey will want to leave soon."

He nods, but doesn't move. "Grace—"

"It's fine, Evan." I walk past him toward the stairs, pausing at the doorway. "We can still go skating. For her sake. But after today..." I turn back to look at him one last time. "Well, I need you to decide what you actually want. Because I can't keep doing this back and forth bullshit. We're too old for it."

I leave him standing in the kitchen, and as I climb the stairs, I hear Lyndsey's excited chatter about her skating boots. Despite everything, I smile. Today I'll focus on what matters most—watching my daughter's face light up on the ice, holding her hands as she wobbles and laughs, being present for the joy that exists right in front of me.

My daughter's love is always enough. It's pure and honest and everything I need.

It's Evan's love that might never be.

Six

The call comes three days after our ice skating trip, while I'm folding laundry and Lyndsey's at school.

"Grace?" Yvette's voice is hesitant on the other end, which is unusual for her. She's never hesitant about anything.

"Hi, Yvette. Is everything okay?" I set down the shirt I was folding, surprised she's calling me directly instead of going through Penny or one of the other family members.

"Yes, everything's fine. I was wondering if... well, if we could talk. About my wedding."

I blink. "Your wedding?"

"Yep! Me and Max are planning it for this spring." There's a warmth in her voice when she says his name that I've rarely heard before. "And I was hoping—that is, Max and I were both hoping—that Lyndsey could be our flower girl."

I sit down heavily on the couch, genuinely touched. "Oh, Yvette. She would be thrilled. Are you sure?"

"Of course I'm sure." Her voice gets softer. "She's family, Grace. And... I know things have been complicated between all of us, especially since Stefan died. But Max thinks the world of her, and so do I."

There's something in her tone. An olive branch, maybe, or an acknowledgment of all the tension that's existed between us. My throat tightens unexpectedly.

"I think she'd love that," I manage. "When were you thinking?"

"March. We wanted something small, just family and close friends. Nothing too elaborate." She pauses. "And Grace? I want to apologize for what I said at the hospital about you and Evan. I was grieving and angry and I took it out on you when you were grieving, too."

I close my eyes, remembering that awful night. "We all said things we didn't mean."

"Maybe. But I meant what I said then, and I was wrong." She takes a breath. "I've been thinking a lot about what Stefan would have wanted. And he wouldn't have wanted his family torn apart by grief."

"No," I agree quietly. "He wouldn't have."

"So... Lyndsey will be in the wedding? I promise we'll make it fun for her."

"Of course. She's going to be over the moon." I smile, imagining my daughter's excitement. "When do you want to tell her?"

"Soon. Maybe this weekend? Max and I could come by, if that's okay."

"That sounds perfect." I pause. "Yvette? Thank you. For including her. For... everything."

"Thank you for saying yes. I'll call you later in the week to work out the details."

After we hang up, I sit there for a moment, surprised by how much lighter my chest feels. It's been so long since anything with the Pierce family felt uncomplicated.

My phone buzzes with a text from Evan:

> Flying to Chicago tomorrow for a conference. Back Friday.

I stare at the message, the sudden lightness disappearing.

Three days. Three days since our conversation in the kitchen, since I laid everything on the line and asked him to fight for us. And his response is to leave town.

Some things never change.

THE GROCERY STORE on Wednesday afternoon is blissfully quiet, which means I can actually think while I shop instead of dodging other carts and waiting in long lines. I'm debating between two different pasta sauces when a deep voice behind me says, "The marinara's better than the meat sauce, if you're looking for a recommendation."

I turn to find a man about my age with medium brown-blond hair and an easy smile, holding a basket with what looks like the ingredients for a proper home-cooked meal.

Not frozen dinners and cereal like half my cart because I'm a terrible cook.

"You've tried both?" I ask, holding up the jars.

"Unfortunately, yes. I've been working my way through every pre-made sauce in town since I moved here." He extends his hand. "I'm Jake, by the way."

"Grace." His handshake is firm and warm. "New to town, I take it?"

"Three weeks now. Took a job at the bank downtown." He grins. "Still figuring out where to find the best of everything. Food, coffee, places that aren't completely dead on a Wednesday night."

I laugh. "Well, I'm afraid I can't help you with the Wednesday night scene. I haven't been out on a weeknight in... well, years."

"Kids?" he asks, and there's no judgment in his voice, just genuine curiosity.

"One. A five-year-old daughter who thinks bedtime is merely a suggestion."

"Five is a fun age. I bet she keeps you busy."

"That's putting it mildly." I toss the marinara into my cart, taking his recommendation. "What brought you to our little corner of the world? It's not exactly a banking metropolis."

"Sometimes that's exactly what you need. I was in Denver before this, and it was all noise and rush and never having time to actually talk to people in grocery stores." He pauses. "Plus my sister lives about an hour away, so it's nice to be closer to family."

There's something refreshing about his openness, the way he talks like we've known each other longer than five minutes. It's been so long since I've had a conversation with someone new, someone who doesn't know my history or have opinions about my choices.

"So what's the verdict on our little town so far?" I ask.

"Still deciding. The people seem friendly, the pace is definitely slower, and the scenery's not bad." His eyes meet mine briefly before he looks away with a slight smile. "Though I have to admit, I don't have much of a social life yet. Still figuring out where people go to meet other people."

"That's easy. The café for breakfast gossip, the library for book clubs, and Murphy's Bar if you're looking for something stronger than coffee."

"Good to know. Though I was thinking more along the lines of dinner somewhere that doesn't involve listening to other people's conversations." He shifts his weight, suddenly looking less confident. "Maybe tomorrow night?"

The question catches me completely off guard. It's been so long since anyone has asked me out that I almost don't recognize what's happening. My first instinct is to say no, to make some excuse about being busy or not ready or whatever other reason I've used to avoid complications.

But then I think about Evan's text message, about him flying off to Chicago while I sit at home waiting for him to decide what he wants.

I surprise myself by replying, "You know what? I'd like that."

His face lights up. "Really? Great. Is there somewhere you'd recommend?"

"Marcello's has the best Italian food in town, and it's quiet enough that we could actually have a conversation."

"Perfect. Seven o'clock?"

"Seven works." I pull out my phone. "Let me give you my number."

As we exchange information, I can't help but notice how normal this feels. Easy and uncomplicated and refreshingly simple.

"I'll see you tomorrow then," Jake says, backing away with that same easy smile. "And thanks for the local recommendations."

"Anytime," I call after him, and I mean it.

As I finish my shopping, I find myself actually looking forward to tomorrow night. Not because I'm trying to make anyone jealous or prove a point, but because for the first time in months, someone sees me as just Grace. Not Stefan's baby mama, not Evan's complicated situation, not someone's mother first and woman second.

Just me.

I ARRIVE at Marcello's five minutes late, which is actually early for me since I spent twenty minutes trying on three different outfits and then another ten minutes giving the babysitter some new instructions about Lyndsey's bedtime routine.

Jake's already seated at a corner table, and he stands when he sees me approaching. He's traded his casual grocery store look for dark slacks and a light blue button-down that brings out his eyes, and I'm glad I went with the green dress instead of jeans.

"You look beautiful," he says, pulling out my chair.

"Thank you." I sit down, trying to remember the last time someone pulled out my chair. "Sorry I'm a little late. Getting a five-year-old settled with a babysitter is like conducting a small orchestra."

"No worries at all. I was enjoying watching the controlled chaos." He gestures toward the kitchen, where servers are weaving between tables with practiced efficiency. "This place has great energy."

The nervous flutter in my stomach starts to settle as we fall into easy conversation. Jake orders wine without making a big production of it and actually listens to my answers instead of just waiting for his turn to talk.

"So what made you choose banking?" I ask after we've ordered. "It doesn't seem like the most exciting career for someone who moved across the country for a change of pace."

He laughs. "Believe it or not, I actually love numbers. There's something satisfying about making everything balance, about helping people figure out their financial puzzles." He takes a sip of wine. "Plus, every small town needs a good banker, and I like being useful."

"That's refreshingly honest. Most people make their jobs sound more glamorous than they are."

"What about you? What do you do when you're not grocery shopping and wrangling five-year-olds?"

"I work at the courthouse. Records and filing, mostly. Not exactly glamorous either, but it pays the bills and lets me be home when Lyndsey gets out of school."

"Lyndsey. Pretty name."

"Thank you. It was actually her father's choice." The words slip out before I can stop them, and I tense, waiting for the inevitable questions about where her father is now.

But Jake just nods. "He has good taste."

Pretty sure he was complimenting me, I blush, but also the fact there's no prying, no awkward pause. Just acceptance, and I find myself relaxing again.

"Tell me about Denver," I say, changing the subject. "What made you leave?"

"Too much of everything, really. Too much work, too much noise, too much pressure to be someone I wasn't sure I wanted to be." He pauses as the server brings our salads. "I was engaged for a while, and she had very specific ideas about what our life should look like. Big house, fancy car, the right social circle. When I realized I was working sixty-hour weeks just to afford a lifestyle I didn't even want, it seemed like a sign."

"What happened to the engagement?"

"Ended about six months before I moved here. Mutual decision, thankfully. She found someone who wanted the same things she did, and I found the courage to admit I wanted something different."

There's no bitterness in his voice, only quiet honesty, and

I find myself leaning forward slightly. "And what do you want?"

"This, actually." He gestures between us, then around the restaurant. "Good food, good conversation, time to actually get to know someone without feeling like I'm checking boxes on some compatibility list." His eyes meet mine. "What about you? What do you want?"

The question catches me off guard, and I realize no one has asked me that in a very long time. Everyone assumes they know what I want, or what I should want, but no one actually asks.

"Honestly? I'm still figuring that out," I say finally. "For the longest time, I just wanted stability for my daughter. But lately..." I trail off, not sure how to finish that thought.

"Lately?"

"Lately I've been wondering if there might be more. If maybe I deserve more than just stability or what's familiar."

Jake's smile is warm and genuine. "I think you definitely deserve whatever makes you happy."

The way he says it, like he means it, like he's already seen something in me worth more than the bare minimum, makes warmth spread through my chest.

For the first time in months, I feel like myself again. Not someone's ex, complication, or someone waiting for scraps of attention.

Just Grace, having dinner with a man who seems genuinely happy to be here with me.

And that feels pretty wonderful.

Seven

I wake up Friday morning with a smile on my face before I even remember why.

Jake.

The memory of last night washes over me—his easy laugh when I told him about Lyndsey's latest attempt to negotiate a later bedtime, the way he listened when I talked about my work, how natural it felt to be myself without constantly analyzing every word or gesture.

My phone buzzes on the nightstand, and I reach for it expecting to see a message from Evan or maybe my mom.

Instead, it's from Jake:

> Had a wonderful time last night. Hope you did too. Would love to do it again soon.

I find myself grinning at the screen like a teenager. When was the last time someone texted me just to say they had a good time? When was the last time I didn't have to decode hidden meanings or wonder if someone was pulling away?

"Mommy!" Lyndsey's voice carries from her room. "Can we have pancakes?"

"Sure, sweetheart," I call back, still smiling as I get out of bed while trying to determine what to text back.

Our morning routine distracts me, although getting Lyndsey ready for school feels different this morning. Lighter, somehow. After breakfast, she chatters about her art class while I braid her hair, and I find myself actually listening instead of mentally running through my list of worries about Evan.

Then she says, "You seem happy, Mommy," while I'm packing her lunch.

"Do I?"

"Yeah. You're humming."

I realize she's right. I am humming some song I heard on the radio yesterday. "I guess I am happy."

"Good," she says matter-of-factly, then steals a grape from her lunch box.

Before long, I'm hustling her into the car. And after I drop her off at school, I drive through town with the windows down despite the January chill, letting the cold air wake me up fully. Everything looks the same as it did yesterday, but somehow I feel different. More present. More like myself.

My phone buzzes again as I pull up to my job. This time it is Evan:

Flight lands at 2. Can we talk when I get back?

I stare at the message, waiting for the familiar flutter of anxiety, the overthinking that usually comes with any communication from him. But instead, all I feel is a kind of calm clarity.

He wants to talk. Fine. But for the first time, I'm not sitting here desperately hoping he'll say the right thing or finally give me what I need. I'm not building up expectations or preparing myself for disappointment.

I'm just... ready. Ready to hear what he has to say, ready to tell him what I need, and ready to walk away if he can't give it to me.

I text back:

Sure. After dinner. Come by around 6.

I hit send and slip my phone into my pocket, still humming as I head inside to work.

For the first time in months, I'm not afraid of what Evan Pierce might or might not do or say, which feels like freedom from something I had no idea was weighing me down so much.

BY THE TIME we get home, the winter light is already fading, the house dim except for the glow from the kitchen window.

Lyndsey kicks off her shoes and skips down the hall, singing some made-up tune, while I head for the kitchen to start dinner.

Spaghetti tonight—easy, comforting, and with that marinara Jake had sworn by at the store. I pull the jar from the pantry, set a pot of water on the stove, and only then remember my phone still tucked in my bag.

I wince when I see Jake's message from this morning sitting unanswered. No excuses. I thumb out a simple reply:

> Sorry for the late reply—work kept me busy.
> I had a really great time last night too.

I drop pasta into the boiling water, stirring slowly. The phone buzzes almost instantly.

> No worries at all. Been thinking about last
> night myself.

A small, involuntary smile creeps across my face. I reach for the jar, twisting the lid.

Another buzz.

> Any chance I can see you again soon?
> Maybe something different this time—I
> found a little barbecue spot I'd love to try.
> Messy but hopefully worth it.

I laugh softly, pouring the sauce into a pan. Messy but hopefully worth it. So far, there's nothing messy about Jake and I text him back:

> That sounds fun. I'll need to check with my sitter, but I'd love that.

Before I can set the phone down, small footsteps patter into the kitchen. Lyndsey appears with her sleeves already shoved to her elbows. "Can I stir?" she asks, pointing at the pot.

"Sure." I move aside and hand her the spoon. "Careful, it's hot."

She grips the spoon with all the seriousness in the world, tongue poking out between her lips as she stirs.

My phone buzzes again on the counter. I glance at it while keeping one eye on the noodles Lyndsey is enthusiastically swishing around.

> Great. I'll handle the details. You let me know if Saturday or Sunday works better.

The excitement of seeing him again this weekend hums in my chest, a promise.

> I'll let you know later tonight. Thanks, Jake.

"Mommy, I'm good at this," Lyndsey announces proudly, sauce-spattered spoon in hand.

I laugh and ruffle her hair. "You are. I might have to let you cook more since I'm not so great at it."

"You're silly, Mommy. I love your food!"

As the scent of garlic and basil fills the kitchen, I realize this ordinary moment where pasta is boiling, my daughter is praising my basic cooking, and there's a man on the other end of my phone who makes me smile is anything but ordinary. It feels like possibility.

Lyndsey sets the spoon down with a clatter, and I take over before everything turns to mush. She trots back to the table, already laying out mismatched napkins and forks. I glance at my phone again, still sitting on the counter, the last message from Jake glowing at me like a secret.

This weekend.

I want to say yes. I want to text back right now that I'll make it work, but the thought of Evan sitting across from me in less than an hour tugs at the edge of my mind. The contrast is stark—Jake's warmth still humming in my chest while the reminder of Evan feels like a shadow slipping under the door.

"Can we have garlic bread?" Lyndsey asks, jolting me out of my thoughts.

"Of course!" I slide the already prepared slices into the oven.

It's grounding, the rhythm of this small regular day: stirring sauce, setting plates, listening to Lyndsey chatter about school. For once, I don't feel like I'm splitting myself down the middle, half here, half lost in worry. Instead, I can hold both truths at once—Evan and whatever conversation waits for me tonight, and Jake with his easy smile and the promise of something new.

When the food is finally on the table, Lyndsey digs in like she hasn't eaten all day. "This is really good, Mommy."

I smile, twirling pasta around my fork. "It's the sauce. A friend recommended it."

"Is he a nice friend?"

I pause, maybe a beat too long, then nod. "Yeah, he is."

She accepts that answer without question, moving on to talk about how excited she is to wear the pretty dress Yvette got her for the wedding. I listen, actually listen, not just nodding through my own worries.

And somewhere between her happy chatter and the scent of garlic drifting from the oven as I finally pull out the garlic bread, I realize—I'm not afraid of tonight. Nervous, maybe. Uncertain. But not afraid.

Because no matter what Evan says, or doesn't say, I'm already standing on steadier ground than I've ever given myself credit for.

By the time the last of the spaghetti dishes are drying in the rack, I can already feel the weight of six o'clock pressing closer. Lyndsey hums as she colors at the kitchen table, oblivious to the quiet storm building in my chest. My phone sits on the counter beside me, the last text from Jake glowing like a promise I'm not ready to say out loud.

I want to grab onto it, cling to the ease and warmth he offers, but I know better than to walk into tonight distracted. Evan won't let me. He never has.

At 5:58, the doorbell rings.

Lyndsey's head shoots up. "I'll get it!"

She dashes for the door before I can stop her, flinging it open with a squeal. "Uncle Evan!"

I wipe my hands on a towel, steadying myself before I step into the entryway. Evan crouches, sweeping her into his arms with practiced ease, laughing as if nothing in the world has ever been complicated between us.

"Hey, Lyndsey. You miss me?"

"Yes!" she beams, clinging to his neck. "We had spaghetti. Mommy let me stir!"

"Lucky girl." He sets her down gently, straightening as his gaze finds mine.

The easy grin doesn't falter, but I catch the flicker beneath it—something measured, careful. He looks good, as always, travel-worn in a way that only seems to add to his appeal and his hair is mussed like he's been running a hand through it all day.

"Grace." His voice is warm, familiar. "Thanks for letting me come by."

I nod, folding my arms loosely. "Of course. Come in."

Lyndsey grabs his hand immediately, tugging him toward the living room. "Will you help me build my Lego house? It's gonna have three bedrooms and a slide."

He chuckles, letting her drag him a few steps before glancing back at me. "I'd love to. If that's okay with you."

There it is again—the charm, the way he steps so easily into this role when it suits him. And maybe once upon a time, that would've been enough to make my chest ache with longing. Now, though, it merely makes me tired.

"Go ahead." I force a small smile for Lyndsey's sake. "I'll make some coffee."

I turn toward the kitchen, needing the space, needing the ritual of measuring grounds and pouring water to steady my hands. I hear Lyndsey's laughter bubbling through the doorway, Evan's deep voice weaving into hers, and for a moment I close my eyes, bracing myself.

Because I know what's coming when the laughter fades and the real conversation begins.

IT DOESN'T TAKE LONG for Lyndsey to get distracted and wander off to her room, which is when Evan locates me sitting at the kitchen table having a small cup of coffee.

He leans against the doorframe, hands tucked casually into his pockets like he hasn't a care in the world. "You hiding from us in here?"

I take a slow sip, letting the heat warm me, then set the mug down. "Just taking a moment."

His lips curve into that familiar grin as he steps closer. "You always did need your moments. Like every morning, where you won't say two words until you have your coffee."

"That hasn't changed" I reply lightly, though my eyes stay steady on him.

He pulls out the chair across from me, lowering himself into it. For a second, neither of us says anything. The only sound is the faint hum of Lyndsey talking to her dolls down the hall.

Evan clears his throat. "Grace, about earlier… about us. I don't want you to think I'm not serious."

My fingers trace the rim of the mug. "Then tell me you are."

"I'm here, aren't I?" His gaze locks on mine, intent but edged with defensiveness.

"You've said that before." I shake my head slowly. "Being here for a night, or a day, or even a weekend—that isn't the same as staying. You swoop in, you remind me of everything we had, and then…" I trail off, lifting my hands helplessly.

He exhales, leaning back in his chair. "I don't mean for it to feel like that."

"But it does," I say softly. "Every time."

The weight between us grows heavier, thick with all the words we've swallowed in the past. I can see him searching for the right thing to say, the magic phrase that will undo years of half-promises and quiet disappearances.

And for once, I don't feel the urge to rescue him from the silence.

"I don't know what you want from me."

Evan's voice is quiet, almost defeated, but there's still an edge to it, like he's bracing for a fight.

I wrap my hands around the warm mug, holding it steady. "I want what I've always wanted. Consistency. Something real. Not just the good days when it's easy to show up."

His jaw tightens. "You think I don't want that, too?"

"I don't know what you want, Evan." My words come out sharper than I intend, but I don't take them back. "You say one thing, you do another. And in between, I'm left trying to explain to my daughter why the man she calls Uncle Evan drifts in and out of her life like a shadow."

He flinches, barely, but I see it.

"You know why it's complicated," he says, his tone raw now. "Every time I look at her, Grace… every time—I see my brother. And how he's missing it all."

I swallow hard, my throat tight. "I know. I see him in her too. Every single day. But I don't get to use that as a reason to pull back. She doesn't get less of me because of what hurts."

He drags a hand through his hair, eyes darting away. "It's not that simple."

"It *is* that simple," I insist, leaning forward. "She needs you, or she doesn't. I need you, or I don't. But what I can't keep doing is waiting for you to decide whether loving us and becoming a family is what you want."

The silence stretches, heavy and suffocating. Lyndsey's laughter floats down the hall, pure and unbothered.

For the briefest moment, I think I see something break across Evan's face—guilt, longing, fear all tangled together. But then he blinks it away, retreating behind that wall he's so good at building.

"Grace…" His voice is low, strained. "I don't know if I can be who you want me to be."

My heart aches, but there's no anger in me anymore—only clarity. I stand, carrying my mug to the sink. "Then maybe it's time you stop trying to be anything at all, except honest."

"You're right."

His voice sounds raspy, like he's choking back words or feelings he refuses to share, but I can't look at him as I say, "You should go, Evan. I don't want to do this anymore, no matter how much it hurts, because both Lyndsey and I deserve more."

There's a brief moment where he sucks in a sharp breath and I wait… wait to feel his hands on my shoulders, for him to turn me around and kiss me and tell me he loves me and he's never letting me go.

That doesn't happen.

I listen to the low rumble of his voice from down the hall as he tells Lyndsey he's tired from his trip and is going home, then… the sound of his footsteps softly against the wooden floors as he heads toward the front door.

No goodbye for me as the door shuts softly behind him.

A single tear escapes, but I swipe it away and pick up my phone, reaching out to see if the babysitter can watch Lyndsey for me this weekend because I don't plan to spend another moment of my life waiting on Evan ever again.

eight

SATURDAY EVENING ARRIVES FASTER THAN I EXPECTED, AND so here I stand in front of my closet for the second time this week, trying to decide what to wear for an evening out with Jake.

"Mommy, you look pretty," Lyndsey says from my doorway, where she's been watching me debate between a blue sweater and a cream-colored blouse.

"Thank you, sweetheart." I settle on the cream blouse because I love how well it suits my coloring. "Remember, the babysitter will be here soon, and you need to be good for her."

"I'm always good," she protests with a grin that suggests otherwise.

"Uh-huh." I kiss the top of her head. "Bedtime is at eight, no negotiating."

The doorbell rings just as I'm applying a final coat of lip gloss, and my stomach does a little flip. It's been so long since

I felt this kind of anticipation—the good kind, not the anxious waiting I'm used to with Evan.

My neighbor who babysits occasionally arrives right on time and I'm grateful for her no-nonsense approach to watching Lyndsey. No twenty questions about where I'm going or who I'm seeing, only a warm smile and a promise to call if anything comes up.

Jake shows up a few minutes later and the sight of him right outside my front door makes me pause in the doorway. He's wearing dark jeans and a gray pullover, nicely complimenting my outfit, and his whole face has brightened upon seeing me.

"You look incredible," he says, holding out his arm for me to take.

"Thank you. So do you." And I mean it. There's something about the way he carries himself—confident but not cocky, relaxed in his own skin—that draws me in.

"I thought we could drive a little out of town," he says, opening the passenger door of his sedan upon reaching it. "There's a little place called The Garden Room that my sister recommended. She says they have live music on Saturday nights."

"I've never been there," I admit as he closes the door and walks around to the driver's side. "But I love music."

"What kind?" he asks, starting the engine.

"Pretty much everything. Though I have a soft spot for acoustic guitar and anything with good lyrics." I settle back in the seat, surprised by how comfortable his car feels. Clean but lived-in, with a coffee cup in the holder and a book on banking regulations in the back seat that makes me smile.

"Good to know. The band tonight is supposed to be folky, so we might be in luck."

The drive takes about twenty minutes, and I'm amazed by how easily conversation flows between us. Jake tells me about the last two days, asking genuine questions about my day on Friday, and somehow we end up talking about books and movies and whether pineapple belongs on pizza.

"Absolutely not," I say firmly when he brings up the controversial topic. "That's just wrong."

"See, I knew I liked you," he laughs. "My ex used to order Hawaiian pizza every time, and I'd pick off the pineapple and suffer in silence."

"That sounds like a fundamental incompatibility right there," I tease, and he grins.

"Should have been my first red flag."

The Garden Room turns out to be exactly the kind of place I would have chosen myself. It's cozy and warm, with exposed brick walls covered in local artwork and soft lighting from vintage fixtures. The hostess seats us at a small table near the stage area, where a duo with acoustic guitars is setting up their equipment.

"This is perfect," I tell Jake as we settle in with our menus. "How did your sister know about this place?"

"She used to date a guy who played here sometimes. Said it was the one good thing that came out of that relationship." He takes a sip of the water we both asked for. "What about you? Any places like this in town that I should know about?"

"Not really. Most of our nightlife consists of the bar I told you about, which is more about beer and pool than ambiance." I glance around the room, taking in the intimate atmosphere. "I forgot how much I missed this."

"Going out?"

"No, just... being somewhere new. Somewhere that doesn't come with a history." The words slip out before I can stop them, and I feel heat rise in my cheeks. "Sorry, that probably sounds dramatic."

"Not at all," Jake says quietly. "Small towns can feel pretty claustrophobic sometimes. Everyone knows everyone, and everyone has opinions about everything."

I look up at him, surprised by the understanding in his voice. "Exactly."

The musicians start their first set, and we fall into comfortable silence, listening to a beautiful cover of an old James Taylor song. Jake's fingers tap quietly against his glass in rhythm with the music, and when the singer hits a particularly lovely note, he catches my eye and smiles.

During the break between sets, our food arrives and we talk more while eating about his move from Denver and then Lyndsey's upcoming role as flower girl in Yvette's wedding.

"So this Yvette," Jake says, cutting into his chicken. "She's your daughter's aunt?"

"Yes." I take a bite of salmon, thinking about how to explain the Pierce family dynamics. "And the whole family is... well, they've been part of Lyndsey's life since she was born."

"That must be nice for her, having that extended family."

"It is," I agree. "Though it can get complicated sometimes with the whole small town thing, as we both know."

"Absolutely," Jake says with a knowing smile. "Dating as a single parent must come with all kinds of complications I can't even imagine."

What strikes me is that he doesn't press for details about Lyndsey's father, doesn't ask probing questions about why I'm single or what happened. Just accepts what I'm willing to share and moves on.

When the second set starts, the musicians play a slow, bluesy number that makes the whole room feel more intimate. Jake leans closer to hear something I'm saying about Lyndsey's latest art project, and I catch a hint of his cologne—something clean and woodsy that makes me want to lean in further.

"Would you like to take a walk?" he asks when the song ends. "I saw a little garden area out back when we came in."

Even though it's a little cold, I definitely don't want the night to end yet. "That sounds nice."

The garden turns out to be a small courtyard strung with tiny white lights, with a few benches scattered among potted plants and a small fountain in the center. It is chilly, but not uncomfortably so, especially when Jake offers me his jacket as I shiver slightly.

"I'm fine," I start to say, but he's already shrugging out of it.

"Please. My mother would disown me if she knew I let a lady get cold." He drapes it around my shoulders, and the gesture is so old-fashioned and sweet it makes my heart beat a bit faster.

We find a bench near the fountain, and I pull his jacket closer around me, breathing in that same clean scent. "Tell me more about your family," I say. "You mentioned a sister."

"Claire. She's three years older and thinks she knows everything about my life." His tone is affectionate. "She's the one who convinced me to take the job here, actually. Said I needed to get out of the city and remember how to be human again."

"Was she right?"

"So far, so good," he says, and when he looks at me, there's something in his expression that makes my breath catch. "Definitely so far, so good. What about yours?"

"Oh, I have my mom, but she doesn't live close so I only see her occasionally. Otherwise, it's just me and Lyndsey."

"I see."

We sit in comfortable silence for a moment, listening to the soft splash of the fountain and the muted music drifting from inside. Jake's sitting close enough I can feel the warmth radiating from his body, and when he shifts slightly, his knee brushes against mine.

"Grace," he says softly.

I turn to look at him, and suddenly the space between us feels charged with possibility. His hand moves to rest on the bench between us, close enough to touch if I wanted to.

"I really like spending time with you," he says. "I know we haven't known each other, and I don't want to assume anything, but..."

"But?" My voice comes out barely above a whisper.

"I'd really like to see where this goes. What about you?"

I let my hand slide over to cover his. His fingers are warm and slightly rough, and when he turns his palm up to link our fingers together, it feels like the most natural thing in the world.

"I'd like that too," I manage.

We stay like that for a while, hands linked, talking quietly about everything and nothing. He tells me about his plans to maybe get a dog once he's more settled, and I tell him about how Lyndsey wanted to become a vet at one point so she could "fix all the sick puppies" before she moved on to wanting to be an astronaut.

When we finally head back inside, our hands stay connected, and I'm amazed by how right it feels. Not desperate or needy or fraught with complications, just... right.

The drive back to my house passes too quickly, filled with more easy conversation and the comfortable weight of his jacket still around my shoulders. When he pulls into my driveway, I'm almost sorry the evening has to end.

"Thank you," I say as he walks me to the front door. "Tonight was wonderful."

"For me too." He stops at the bottom of the porch steps, still holding my hand. "Grace?"

"Yes?"

"I don't want to overstep, but..." He takes a step closer, and my heart skips a beat. "I'd like to kiss you goodnight."

The request is so gentle, so respectful, that it takes my breath away as I whisper, "I'd like that."

He steps up onto the first porch step, bringing us to almost the same height, and lifts his free hand to cup my cheek. For a moment, we stare at each other, and I can see the same wonder in his eyes that's singing through my veins.

When his lips finally touch mine, it's soft and sweet and perfect. No desperate hunger or urgent need, only a gentle exploration that makes me feel cherished. His thumb traces across my cheekbone as he deepens the kiss slightly, and I find myself leaning into him, my free hand coming up to rest against his chest.

When we finally break apart, we're both breathing a little unsteadily, and I can see the same dazed expression on his face that I'm sure is on mine.

"Wow," he says softly.

"Yeah," I agree, unable to keep the smile off my face. "Wow."

He kisses my forehead gently, then steps back, though he doesn't let go of my hand. "I'll call you tomorrow."

"Okay, good."

He squeezes my hand once more before reluctantly releasing it. "Sweet dreams, Grace."

I watch him walk back to his car, raising my hand in a small wave when he looks back before getting in. As his taillights disappear down the street, I touch my lips with my fingers, still feeling the warmth of his kiss.

Inside, the babysitter reports that Lyndsey went to bed without argument and slept soundly. After I pay her and she leaves, I find myself wandering around my quiet house, Jake's jacket still draped over my shoulders.

I catch sight of myself in the hallway mirror and pause. The woman looking back at me has bright eyes and flushed cheeks, and she looks... happy. Not the careful, guarded happiness I've practiced for so long, but the real thing.

For the first time in years, I'm looking forward to tomorrow. Not because I'm hoping someone else will finally give me what I need, but with genuine excitement about what might come next.

nine

THREE WEEKS LATER, I STAND IN FRONT OF MY BATHROOM mirror applying mascara as my phone buzzes with a text from Jake.

I smile at the screen, warmth spreading through my chest. Six dates, and he still manages to make me feel like a teenager with a crush. Tonight will be the first time I'm going to his place - a small rental house on the outskirts of town that he's been slowly making his own.

I set the phone down and take one last look in the

mirror. The dark green dress I chose brings out my eyes, and for once, I feel genuinely pretty instead of just trying to look acceptable. These regular dates with Jake have done something to my confidence that I didn't expect.

We've taken things slow with dinners, a movie, long walks around the lake, and coffee dates when I can grab a free hour sometimes. Nothing beyond sweet kisses goodnight and the comfortable warmth of holding hands, but every moment with him has felt easy and natural in a way I'd long ago forgotten was possible.

"Mommy!" Lyndsey calls from downstairs. "Mimi is here!"

"Coming!" I grab my purse and cardigan, excitement bubbling in my stomach. Jake promised to cook for me tonight, and something about the gesture with him wanting to take care of me in his space feels significant.

I'm halfway down the stairs when there's a sharp knock at the front door. The babysitter is already inside, hanging up her coat, and Lyndsey is showing her the puzzle she's been working on at the kitchen table.

"I'll get it," I call, wondering who the heck would be arriving at this time of night.

I'm not surprised, for some reason, that Evan's standing on my front porch, his hands shoved deep in his jacket pockets and his jaw set in the familiar line that screams he's angry about something.

"We need to talk," he says without preamble.

My stomach drops. "Evan, I'm on my way out."

"To see Jake Morrison." It's not a question, and the way he says Jake's name makes it sound like a curse word.

I glance over my shoulder toward the kitchen where Mimi and Lyndsey are chatting, then step outside, pulling the door partially closed behind me. "What?"

"Small town, Grace. Did you really think no one would notice you having dinner dates all over the county?" His eyes are darker than usual, and there's something almost desperate in his expression that I've never seen before.

I want to laugh at his description yet don't as I say carefully, heart racing, "I wasn't hiding anything. And I don't owe you an explanation about who I spend time with."

"Don't I get a say in this? In who's around my niece?"

The possessive edge to his voice makes me take a step back, scowling at him. "Your niece? Since when do you get to make decisions about Lyndsey's life ? Did you also forget you've barely been in it for the past year and a half?"

"That's not fair."

"Isn't it?" I cross my arms, suddenly grateful for the confidence Jake has helped me find. "You can't disappear when things get complicated and then show up demanding control when I start moving on."

"Moving on?" He moves closer, and I can smell the familiar scent of his cologne that used to make my knees weak. "Is that what this is? Some kind of revenge?"

"God, Evan, not everything is about you." The words come out sharper than I intended, yet I don't take them back. "Maybe I'm dating Jake because I like him. Maybe I'm dating him because he actually wants to spend time with me without it being some complicated secret or emotional minefield."

Something flickers across his face; hurt, maybe, or surprise. "Grace... I—"

"No." I hold up a hand to stop him. "You had your chance. Multiple chances. I told you what I needed from you, and instead of fighting for us, it's been radio silence for three weeks."

"I was giving you space."

"I didn't want or need space, Evan. That's you. What I wanted was for you to prove that I'm worth fighting for. That we are worth fighting for." My voice is rising slightly, and I force myself to lower it. "But you haven't done a damn thing. So I've stopped waiting."

He runs a hand through his hair in that familiar gesture, but this time instead of making me want to comfort him, it just makes me tired.

"Look." I glance at my watch. "I told you I'm on my way out. If you want to talk about this, we can do it another time. But I'm not canceling my plans to have the same conversation we've been having for three years."

"You're really going to choose him over me?"

The question hangs in the air between us, and I can see in his eyes that he genuinely expects me to drop everything and focus on his feelings, the way I always have.

But after weeks of Jake's steady presence, of someone who shows up when he says he will and doesn't make me guess where I stand, I know what I've been settling for and I'm not doing it any longer.

"I'm not choosing him over you, Evan," I say quietly. "I'm choosing me."

I step back toward the door, my hand on the handle. "If you want to be part of my life, you know where to find me. But I'm not waiting around anymore while you figure out what you want."

His mouth opens like he wants to say something else as I'm already turning away, slipping back inside before he can respond.

Mimi looks up from the puzzle as I lean against the closed door, my heart pounding. "Everything alright?"

"Fine," I manage, though my hands are shaking slightly. "Just... an unexpected visitor."

Through the window, I can see Evan still standing on the porch for a long moment before finally walking back to his car. I watch his taillights disappear down the street, and instead of the usual hollow ache in my chest, I feel something else entirely.

Relief.

And underneath that, excitement for the evening ahead with someone who actually wants to be there.

"Okay," I say, smoothing down my dress and grabbing my purse. "I should be back by eleven at the latest. Lyndsey's bedtime is eight, and there are snacks in the pantry if she gets hungry. Thank you so much."

"My pleasure," Mimi says with a knowing smile. "Have a good time!"

Which is exactly what I intend to do as I push Evan out

of my mind and head to Jake's to see what he's got in store for us tonight.

———————

Jake's house is exactly what I expected; clean but comfortable, with books stacked on every available surface and a kitchen that actually looks lived-in rather than staged. The dinner he made was incredible—garlic herb chicken with roasted vegetables that he clearly spent hours preparing.

"You really didn't have to go to all this trouble," I tell him as we clear the plates from his small dining table.

"I wanted to," he says simply, loading dishes into the dishwasher. "Besides, I like cooking for people, just haven't had anyone to cook for in a while."

The casual honesty in his voice makes my chest warm. There's something so refreshing about being with someone who says exactly what they mean without layers of hidden meaning to decode.

"Well, it was amazing. I can barely manage spaghetti without burning something." Rinsing a wine glass, I'm hyperaware of how domestic this feels, the two of us moving around his kitchen together like we've done this a hundred times before.

"I doubt that's true," Jake says, bumping my shoulder gently as he reaches around me for a dish towel. "You strike me as someone who's good at everything she puts her mind to."

I turn to look at him, and suddenly the space between us

feels charged. He's close enough that I can see the flecks of green in his blue eyes, close enough that when he reaches up to tuck a strand of hair behind my ear, I feel the warmth of his fingers against my cheek.

"Grace," he says softly, and there's a question in his voice that makes my breath catch.

Instead of answering with words, I lean into his touch, letting my eyes drift closed for a moment. When I open them again, he's looking at me with an expression that's equal parts tender and hungry.

"Is this okay?" he asks, his other hand coming up to frame my face.

"Yes," I whisper, and then his lips are on mine.

This kiss is different from our gentle goodnights on my front porch. Deeper, more insistent, with three weeks of careful restraint finally giving way to something more urgent. My hands find the front of his shirt, fisting in the soft cotton as he backs me gently against the kitchen counter.

His hands slide down to my waist, pulling me closer, and I can feel the solid warmth of his body against mine. When his lips move to trail along my jaw, I hear myself make a soft sound I barely recognize.

"I've been wanting to do this," he murmurs against my ear, his voice rough in a way that sends heat straight through me.

"Oh yeah?" I manage, tilting my head to give him better access to my neck.

"Mmhmm. And you're worth waiting for Grace." He

pulls back to look at me with those impossibly sincere eyes. "If you're not ready, no pressure."

The simple honesty of it with no games, no manipulation, and genuine care for my feelings, nearly undoes me completely.

"I am," I whisper, wanting to experience this man in a completely new way that I'm sure will feel as good as everything else.

He leads me upstairs, holding my hand the entire time, and pulls me flush against him once we enter the room.

We stare into each other's eyes as he starts unbuttoning my blouse and in return, I tug his shirt free from his jeans. Piece after piece of clothing is removed from both our bodies until we're both naked. He looks me up and down, grins, then captures my lips with his before picking me up in his arms and carrying me to the bed.

He's so gentle, sliding his hands across my skin and caressing every inch of me he can reach, all while our tongues tangle in a passionate dance. But there's also an urgency between us.

I feel him hard between my legs and I'm already so turned on that all I can think about is getting closer. I slide a hand between our bodies and his groan as I wrap my hand around him is delicious, deep and guttural as if he hasn't been touched like this in a while.

His lips leave mine and I feel him staring at me for a second before his eyes slam shut while I slide my hand toward the tip of him, then down again. He adjusts a little then and his hand in between my legs, causing me to gasp and my skin to flush as he touches me intimately.

He kisses me again, whispering, "Tell me what works best for you," even as he slides his finger to my clit, gently moving his finger around it. When I simply lift my hips into his touch, he laughs softly and firms his touching, moving his lips to a nipple begging for his attention.

His expert touching leads me fast toward an orgasm, and as I'm reeling from its intensity, he adjusts on top of me and I watch as he reaches toward the nightstand. He slips a condom on, moves back into position, and devours my mouth with his for a few brief moments before saying, "Wrap your legs around me, beautiful."

I do, and he grips one leg while pushing inside me both of us gasping when he's fully in. The moment is everything I thought it would be and we cling to each other while moving together in what feels like perfect harmony. There's no awkwardness, just an ease between us… right to the end.

Afterward, we lie tangled together, my head on his chest as his fingers trace lazy patterns on my bare shoulder. His room is dim except for the soft glow from the hallway light, and I feel more relaxed than I have in years.

"You okay?" Jake asks softly, pressing a kiss to the top of my head.

"More than okay," I say, tilting my face up to look at him. "That was…wonderful."

"Yeah," he agrees with a smile that makes me want to kiss him all over again. "It really was."

We stay like that for a while, talking quietly about everything and nothing. He tells me about his favorite places in Denver that he misses, and I tell him about the time Lyndsey convinced me to let her paint her bedroom walls with finger paints because she wanted to "make it beautiful for when Daddy came to visit."

"You've mentioned him a few times in past tense," he observes softly before asking gently, "How old was she when he died?" His fingers continue moving in soothing circles on my skin.

"She had just turned four a few weeks before." I pause, surprised by how easy it is to talk about this with him. "She always asks about him still. Wonders why he can't come back."

"That must be hard for both of you."

"It is. But she's resilient. Kids are amazing that way." I trace a pattern of my own on his chest with my finger. "Did you ever think about having kids?"

"Well, my ex wasn't interested, and honestly, I've never been sure I'm ready." He's quiet for a moment. "But spending time with you and hearing about Lyndsey... I think about it quite a bit now."

The casual way he includes himself in my future, in Lyndsey's life, should probably scare me. Instead, it fills me with a warmth I wasn't expecting.

"She'd like you," I say. "She's been asking about me going out lately."

"Smart kid." He shifts slightly so he can see my face better. "Grace?"

"Mmm?"

"I know we're taking this slow, and I'll never push you, but…" He pauses, seeming to choose his words carefully. "I want you to know that I'm serious about you. I'm not going anywhere."

The simple declaration should fill me with warmth, and it does… however, underneath that comfort, something twists uncomfortably in my chest. The certainty in his voice, the way he looks at me like I'm exactly what he's been searching for, makes me feel suddenly exposed.

Because as much as I care about Jake, as right as this feels, there's still a part of me that jumps every time my phone buzzes, hoping it might be Evan finally ready to fight for us.

"Good," I manage, reaching up to kiss him softly, trying to push the doubt away. "Because I'm not planning on going anywhere either."

Yet even as I say the words, while Jake's arms tighten around me in response, I can't shake the feeling I'm making a promise I may not be prepared to keep.

Not because I don't want to be here with him, but because some small, stubborn part of my heart is still waiting for Evan Pierce to decide I'm worth the risk.

And that realization makes me feel like the worst kind of person.

ten

Five days after my night with Jake, I'm sitting at my
kitchen table staring at two different text conversations on
my phone, feeling like I'm being pulled in opposite
directions.

Jake's messages are exactly what I've come to expect from
him - consistent, sweet, and uncomplicated:

> Good morning, Grace. Hope you slept well.

> Thinking about you. Can't wait to see you
> again.

> How's your day going? Lyndsey doing okay
> in school?

Then there's Evan, frustrating me with how… desperate
he seems to make me talk to him when I've done too much
talking already:

> We need to finish our conversation.

> I was wrong to just show up like that. Can we talk?

> Grace, please. I know I messed up.

I set the phone down with a sigh, rubbing my temples where a dull headache has been building for the past two days. I've been feeling off—tired, slightly nauseous, like I'm coming down with something. The last thing I need is to deal with Evan's sudden urgency to talk while fighting off what feels like the flu.

"Mommy, you look bad," Lyndsey observes from across the table, where she's eating cereal before school.

"Thanks, sweetheart. Very flattering." I force a smile, though she's not wrong. I caught sight of myself in the bathroom mirror this morning and immediately thought I looked pale and drawn.

"Are you sick?"

"Maybe a little. Nothing serious." I reach over to smooth her hair. "Finish your cereal so we're not late."

My phone buzzes again; it's Jake this time.

> You've been more quiet than I'm used to these past couple days. Everything okay?

The genuine concern in his message makes my chest tighten with guilt. I should respond, should let him know I'm fine, just not feeling well. But every time I start to type something back, I find myself staring at Evan's messages instead.

I know I messed up.

Why does it seem he's finally saying the right things now, when I'm trying so hard to move forward?

"Mommy?" Lyndsey's voice pulls me back to the present. "Can I wear my flower girl dress to school?"

"What? No, honey, that's for Aunt Yvette's wedding. Remember?" I blink, trying to focus on her instead of the competing voices in my head. "Your regular clothes are fine."

She pouts but doesn't argue, and I realize I need to get it together. Whatever's going on with me... this bug I'm fighting, the confusion about Evan and Jake... Lyndsey doesn't deserve to deal with a distracted, irritable mother.

After I drop her off at school, I sit in the car for a few minutes, feeling another wave of that queasy, unsettled feeling wash over me. Maybe I should go home and rest instead of going to work. I haven't called in sick in months, and honestly, I feel worse now than I did this morning.

My phone rings, Jake's name on the screen.

"Hello?" I try to inject some energy into my voice, but it doesn't work.

"Hey, you sound tired. You okay?"

There's that care again, that immediate concern for my wellbeing that should make me feel grateful instead of conflicted.

"I think I'm getting sick," I admit. "Been feeling pretty rough the past couple days."

"Oh no. Have you been to the doctor?"

"It's probably a bug, something Lyndsey brought home from school. I'll be fine in a few days."

"Are you sure? I could bring you soup, or medicine, or..." He pauses. "Sorry, am I being overbearing? I only want to take care of you."

And there it is, the difference between Jake and Evan laid out in one simple statement. Jake wants to take care of me. Evan's always wanted me to take care of him.

"You're not being overbearing," I say softly. "You're being sweet. But I think I just need rest."

"Okay. Call me if you need anything. And I mean anything, Grace."

"I promise I will. Thank you, Jake."

After we hang up, I sit staring at my phone for another few minutes. Jake is everything I thought I wanted—reliable, caring, emotionally available. So why can't I stop thinking about Evan's messages?

Maybe it's because I've spent so long wanting him to fight for me that now that he seems ready to try, I don't know how to let go of that hope.

Or maybe I'm overthinking everything because I feel like garbage.

I drive home instead of going to work, calling in with a migraine that isn't entirely a lie. The headache has gotten worse, and the nauseous feeling keeps coming in waves that leave me gripping the bathroom sink.

By noon, I'm curled up on the couch with a blanket, trying to nap yet unable to turn off my racing thoughts. My phone sits on the coffee table, buzzing occasionally with messages I'm not ready to deal with.

When I finally check it around two, there's another text from Jake checking up on how I'm feeling, and one from Evan that makes my stomach clench:

> I love you. I should have said it weeks ago, months ago. I love you and I was an idiot to let you walk away.

I stare at the words I've been wanting to hear for three years, and instead of the joy I expected to feel, all I feel is tired.

Tired of the back and forth, tired of feeling sick, tired of not knowing what I want or what's right for Lyndsey or whether I'm being unfair to Jake by not being completely present in whatever we're building.

I close my eyes and pull the blanket over my head, hoping that when I wake up, everything will be clearer.

But deep down, I suspect it's only going to get more complicated.

THE SOUND of knocking pulls me out of a deep, dreamless sleep. For a moment, I'm completely disoriented; the living room is dim, and according to the clock on the wall, it's nearly four-thirty.

Four-thirty.

"Oh god," I breathe, scrambling off the couch as the knocking continues. "Lyndsey."

I rush to the door, my head still foggy from sleep, and find Elizabeth standing on my porch with Lyndsey's hand in hers. My daughter looks perfectly fine, chattering away about something, but her expression is concerned.

"Grace? The school called me when you didn't show up for pickup,"she says gently. "Are you okay?"

"I'm so sorry." The words tumble out as I step back to let them in, my cheeks burning with embarrassment. "I fell asleep and I didn't hear my phone and—"

"It's okay," she interrupts, squeezing my arm. "Really. These things happen."

"Mommy, you look funny," Lyndsey announces, studying my face with five-year-old directness. "Your hair is all crazy."

I run a hand over what I'm sure is a disaster, trying to smooth it down. "I was napping, sweetheart. Thank you for being patient."

"Auntie Liz bought me a cookie!" Lyndsey holds up a bag from the bakery downtown. "Can I have it after dinner?"

"Of course." I look at Elizabeth, feeling another wave of that queasy exhaustion. "Thank you. I don't know what happened, I never sleep that hard during the day."

"Why don't you go watch cartoons for a few minutes?" Elizabeth suggests to Lyndsey. "Your mom and I need to talk."

Once Lyndsey settles on the couch with the remote,

Elizabeth follows me to the kitchen, her eyes never leaving my face.

"You look awful," she says bluntly. "And I mean that in the most caring way possible."

"Thanks," I mutter, filling a glass with water. "That's exactly what every woman wants to hear."

"How long have you been feeling sick?"

"A few days. Maybe since Tuesday?" I take a sip of water, hoping it will settle my stomach. "I think I'm just fighting off a bug."

Elizabeth leans against the counter, crossing her arms. "What kind of symptoms?"

"Tired, nauseous, headaches. Classic flu stuff." I shrug, though the movement makes me feel dizzy. "Why are you looking at me like that?"

"Grace." Her voice is gentle but serious. "When was your last period?"

The question hits me like a physical blow. I set down the water glass, my hands suddenly shaking.

"I... I don't..." I try to think back, but everything feels fuzzy. "I've been so stressed with work and everything with Evan, I haven't really been paying attention..."

"Hey." She moves closer, her expression shifting to something like sympathy mixed with concern. "Have you taken a test?"

"A test?" I repeat stupidly, though I know exactly what she means.

"A pregnancy test."

The words hang in the air between us, and suddenly

everything clicks into place with horrible clarity. The exhaustion, the nausea, sleeping through Lyndsey's pickup time, the way certain smells have been bothering me but I brushed aside because that could be the flu too.

It's been a long time since I was pregnant with Lyndsey, but suddenly, the symptoms seem all too familiar.

"Oh god." I sink into one of the kitchen chairs, my legs feeling unable to support me out of nowhere. "Oh shit."

"It's okay," she says quickly, pulling out the chair next to mine. "It might be nothing. But the symptoms..."

"It can't be." My voice sounds distant, like it's coming from someone else. "I mean, it could be, but..."

"Jake?" she asks gently.

I shake my head. "Too recent. It would have to be..." I can't finish the sentence.

"Evan."

I nod, feeling tears prick at my eyes. "New Year's Eve. We didn't... I mean, we should have been more careful, but I stupidly thought..."

"Grace." She reaches over and takes my hand. "Whatever's going on, we'll figure it out. But first, you need to know for sure."

"I can't be pregnant," I whisper. "Not now. Not when everything is so complicated and I'm finally starting to figure things out with Jake and..."

"Grace." Her voice is firm but kind. "One step at a time. Do you want me to go get a test while you stay here with Lyndsey?"

The practical suggestion cuts through my panic. "Would you?"

"Of course." She stands, grabbing her purse. "I'll be back in ten minutes. Try to breathe, okay? Whatever this is, you're not alone."

After she leaves, I sit at the kitchen table listening to the sounds of Lyndsey's cartoon drifting in from the living room. My hands rest on my still-flat stomach, and I try to imagine what another pregnancy would mean.

Another baby. Another tie to the Pierce family. Another complication in an already impossible situation.

And Jake... what would I even say to Jake?

By the time Elizabeth returns with a small pharmacy bag, I've worked myself into a state of barely controlled panic. But her calm presence helps ground me as she hands me the box and points toward the bathroom.

"Three minutes," she says. "I'll watch Lyndsey."

The three longest minutes of my life pass in my tiny bathroom, and when I finally look at the test, the two pink lines are unmistakable.

Pregnant.

I'm pregnant with Evan's baby, and I'm dating another man who has no idea what he's gotten himself into.

When I emerge from the bathroom, Elizabeth takes one look at my face and doesn't need to ask for the results.

"Oh, honey," she says, pulling me into a hug as the tears I've been holding back finally spill over.

And all I can think is: what the hell am I going to do now?

<h1 style="text-align:center">eleven</h1>

I sit in my car outside Jake's house for ten minutes before I finally work up the courage to knock on his door. My hands are shaking, and I've rehearsed what I'm going to say at least twenty different ways during the drive over here.

None of them sound right.

When Jake opens the door, his face immediately brightens, then shifts to concern as he takes in my expression.

"Grace? What's wrong?" He steps back to let me in, his hand automatically moving to the small of my back in that gentle, protective way he has. "You sounded upset in your text."

"I'm sorry for just showing up like this," I begin, but he cuts me off.

"Don't apologize. You know you're always welcome here." He guides me to his couch, sitting down next to me with that same concerned expression. "You're scaring me a little. What's going on?"

I take a shaky breath, trying to find the words. There's no good way to do this, no gentle lead-in that will make what I have to say any easier to hear.

"Jake, I... there's something I need to tell you. About why I've been feeling sick."

He nods, waiting patiently, and I can see him trying to piece together where this is going.

"I'm pregnant," I say quietly.

The words hang in the air between us. Jake's expression goes completely blank for a moment, like he's processing what I just said, and then something that might be hope flickers across his face.

"Pregnant," he repeats slowly.

"Yes." My voice comes out barely above a whisper.

"And..." He pauses, and I can see him doing the math in his head, trying to figure out if there's any possibility. "It's not..."

"No." I close my eyes, hating myself for having to hurt him like this. "It's not yours. We haven't... the timing doesn't work."

Jake goes very still beside me, his hand dropping away from where it had been resting on my knee. When I open my eyes, he's staring straight ahead, his jaw tight.

"Someone else," he says quietly.

"Yes."

"Recently?"

"From before we met," I reply, not trusting my voice to

explain anything else without getting into details I'm not ready to share.

The silence stretches between us, heavy and uncomfortable. I can practically hear Jake's mind working, trying to process this information and figure out what it means for us.

"I'm so sorry," I finally say, the words tumbling out. "I know this isn't what you signed up for when we started seeing each other. I know this complicates everything and I don't expect you to—"

"Grace." His voice is quiet but firm. "Stop."

I fall silent, watching as he runs a hand through his hair and takes a deep breath.

"How long have you known?" he asks finally.

"Since yesterday. A friend helped me figure it out when I fell asleep and missed picking up Lyndsey from school." I twist my hands in my lap. "I've been feeling off all week, but I thought I was just getting sick."

Jake nods slowly, still not looking at me directly. "And... the father? Does he know?"

"No. You're the first person I've told."

That seems to surprise him. He finally turns to look at me, and there's something unreadable in his expression. "Why me first?"

The question catches me off guard. "Because I care about you and we've been dating. Because I didn't want you to hear it from someone else or wonder why I was pulling away." I take a shaky breath. "Because you deserve to know what's happening before we... before this goes any further."

He's quiet for a long moment, staring down at his hands. When he finally speaks, his voice is softer than I expected.

"I care about you too, Grace. A lot more than I probably should after just a few weeks." He looks up at me, and I can see the conflict in his eyes. "But this changes things."

"I know."

"I mean, I knew you had some complicated history. But a baby..." He shakes his head. "That's not just complicated. That's a lifetime connection to someone else."

The stark honesty of it makes my chest tight. "Jake, I don't know what's going to happen. I don't know what any of this means for my future or Lyndsey's or—"

"That's just it," he interrupts gently. "You have to figure that out. And I can't be part of that conversation."

I feel tears starting to build behind my eyes. "So that's it? We're done?"

Jake reaches over and takes my hand, his thumb stroking across my knuckles. "I don't know. Maybe. I honestly don't know what to think right now."

"I understand if you can't handle this," I say, though saying the words feels like swallowing glass. "I know it's a lot to ask—"

"It's not about what I can handle," he says, his voice strained. "It's about what's fair. To you, to me, to that baby." He pauses. "To Lyndsey."

The mention of my daughter makes something twist in my stomach. "What about Lyndsey?"

"Grace, we haven't even... I haven't met her yet. We were taking things slow, getting to know each other first." He releases my hand and leans back against the couch. "And now you're pregnant with another man's baby, a man you clearly still have feelings for, and I'm supposed to what? Pretend that doesn't change the entire dynamic?"

"I never said I still have feelings for him," I protest weakly.

Jake gives me a look that's equal parts sad and knowing. "You don't have to say it. It's written all over your face right now and you look a little guilty."

The truth of that hits me like a physical blow. Am I that transparent?

"I'm sorry," I whisper. "I'm so sorry, Jake. You didn't deserve to get caught up in all this mess."

"Neither did you," he says quietly. "But here we are."

We sit in silence for several minutes, both lost in our own thoughts. Finally, Jake speaks again.

"I think... maybe we need to take a step back. Let you figure out what's happening the baby and everything else." His voice is careful, measured. "And maybe once the dust settles, we can see where we both stand."

It's not the rejection I was bracing for, but it's not the understanding acceptance I was hoping for either. It's something in between—a door left slightly ajar rather than slammed shut.

"Okay," I manage. "I understand."

"Grace." He turns to face me fully, and there's genuine warmth in his eyes despite the hurt I can see there. "For what it's worth, these past few weeks with you have been, well, they've been really good. Under different circumstances..."

"I know," I say, standing up before the tears can start in earnest. "Under different circumstances, things might have been really good for us."

He walks me to the door, and for a moment, we just stand there looking at each other. Then he leans forward and presses a soft, gentle kiss to my forehead.

"Take care of yourself," he says. "And call me if you need anything. I mean that."

I nod, not trusting my voice, and walk back to my car on unsteady legs.

As I drive away, I catch sight of Jake in my rearview mirror, standing in his doorway watching me leave. The image stays with me all the way home, a reminder of what I might have had if my life wasn't so damn complicated.

But there's no point dwelling on might-have-beens. I have a baby coming, a five-year-old to think about, and a conversation with Evan that I can't put off much longer.

Whether I'm ready for it or not.

***

"ARE YOU OKAY?"

The question is from Elizabeth, who I called crying after my visit to Jake's, because I need someone who would understand.

"No," I admit, clutching my phone tighter as I pace around my living room. "I'm really not okay."

"I'm so sorry, Grace. I know that couldn't have been easy."

"He was so understanding. And hurt. And I could see him trying to figure out how to make it work, but knowing he couldn't." I sink onto the couch, exhaustion hitting me like a wave. "God, Liz, what kind of person am I? Jake is everything I thought I wanted, and I've ruined it."

"You haven't ruined anything," she says firmly. "You didn't plan it and you were honest with him as soon as you found out. That's the right thing to do."

"Is it? Because it feels like I'm just making one mess after another." I rub my temples where another headache is starting. "And I still have to tell Evan, and I don't even know how to begin that conversation."

"Have you thought about what you want to say?"

"I don't know what I want, period." The admission comes out more raw than I intended. "I've spent months being angry at him for not fighting for us, and now I'm pregnant with his baby and I don't know if that changes everything or nothing."

"What does your gut tell you?"

I'm quiet for a moment, trying to sort through the chaos in my head. "That I'm scared. That this baby deserves better than parents who can't figure out how to be together without hurting each other."

"Grace—"

"And Lyndsey," I continue, the words spilling out now. "How do I explain this to her? That mommy's having another baby with her daddy's brother, but we're not together?"

"One step at a time," Elizabeth responds gently. "You don't have to have all the answers right now."

"But I do, don't I? I'm going to start showing eventually, and people are going to talk, and the whole Pierce family is going to have opinions about—"

A sharp knock on the front door cuts me off mid-sentence. I freeze, looking toward the entryway.

"Grace? What's wrong?"

"Hold on. Someone's at the door."

I walk toward the door, hoping it's just a delivery or neighbor, but somehow knowing it's not going to be that simple. Through the peephole, I can see Evan standing on my porch, his hands shoved deep in his jacket pockets and that familiar tense set to his shoulders that means he's worked up about something.

"Shit," I breathe, voice barely audible.

"What?"

"It's Evan." My heart starts racing as he knocks again, more insistently this time.

"Grace, I know you're in there," he calls through the door. "Your car's in the driveway and we need to talk."

"Liz, I have to go," I whisper into the phone.

"Are you sure? I could come over—"

"No, I need to handle this myself." Though honestly, I have no idea how I'm going to manage that. "I'll call you later."

I hang up and take a deep breath, trying to compose myself before opening the door. But when I see Evan's face —the frustration and something that looks almost like desperation in his eyes—I realize there's no amount of composing that's going to make this conversation easier.

"You've been ignoring my texts," he says without preamble.

"I've been busy," I reply, not moving to let him in.

"For almost a week? Grace, I told you I love you and you have completely ignored me."

The words hang between us, and I can see in his expression that my silence has been eating at him. Under different circumstances, that might have given me some satisfaction. Now it just makes everything more complicated.

"We need to talk," he continues, his voice softer now. "Please."

I look at him standing there—this man who's been at the center of my world for so long, who's hurt me and disappointed me and who I'm still not sure I can trust with my heart.

This man who's about to become the father of my second child.

"Yes," I say finally, stepping back to let him in. "We really do."

twelve

EVAN STEPS INTO MY LIVING ROOM AND IMMEDIATELY STARTS pacing, the restless energy radiating off him that I remember from our worst arguments. He runs his hands through his hair, stops, then starts pacing again.

"You can't just ignore me, Grace. Not after what I said."

"I wasn't ignoring you," I lie, settling onto the couch because my legs suddenly feel unsteady. "I've been dealing with some things."

"What things?" He stops pacing and looks at me directly for the first time since he walked in. "Are you okay? You look..."

"I look what?"

"Like you haven't been sleeping." His voice softens with genuine concern. "Are you sick?"

The question hits too close to home, and I have to look away. "I'm fine."

"No, you're not." He moves closer, and I catch that familiar scent of his cologne that used to make me feel safe. Now it just makes everything more complicated. "Grace, talk to me."

"You first," I say, buying myself time to figure out how to handle this. "You said you needed to talk."

Evan sits down in the chair across from me, leaning forward with his elbows on his knees. "I meant what I said in my texts. I love you. I should have said it months ago, years ago, but I was scared."

"Scared of what?"

"Of losing you. Of not being good enough. Of screwing up everything with you if… the rest of the family didn't approve, as if that should've mattered." He pauses. "Of admitting that I've been in love with you since shortly after we started seeing each other and feeling guilty about it."

The admission hangs in the air between us. It's what I've wanted to hear for so long, but now that he's saying it, all I can think about is the baby growing inside me and how much more complicated this makes everything.

"You have a funny way of showing love," I say quietly. "Disappearing for eighteen months. Flying out of town when I told you what I needed."

"I know." He scrubs his face with his hands. "I know I handled everything wrong. But knowing you were seeing someone else… it made me realize I'm about to lose the best thing that's ever happened to me."

That doesn't please me as much as I thought it might. "So you only want me now that someone else does?"

"No." His voice is fierce. "I've always wanted you. I was being too much of a coward to fight for you."

I study his face, trying to read the truth in his expression. He looks sincere, desperate even, but I've been down this road with him before.

"What's different now, Evan? What's changed?"

"I have." He stands up and starts pacing again. "Seeing you move on, realizing you might actually be happy without me? It woke me up. I don't want to be the guy who plays it safe anymore. I want to be the guy who deserves you."

"And Jake?"

Evan's jaw tightens at the mention of his name. "What about him?"

"Are you going to be okay with the fact that I've been seeing someone else? That I might have developed feelings for someone else?"

"Have you?" The question comes out sharp, almost accusatory. "Do you have feelings for him?"

I think about Jake's gentle hands, his easy laugh, the way he made me feel worthy of more than scraps and secrets. "Yes," I admit. "I do."

Something flickers across Evan's face—hurt, maybe, or jealousy. "But you're here with me now."

"Because you showed up at my door demanding to talk."

"Because you still love me."

It's not a question, and the certainty in his voice makes my chest tight. Because he's not wrong, and we both know it.

"Love isn't enough, Evan," I say finally. "I've learned that the hard way."

"It's a start though, isn't it?" He moves closer, sitting on the edge of the coffee table so he's right in front of me. "Grace, I know I messed up. I know I hurt you. But I'm here now, and I'm not going anywhere."

Oh… if only I could believe that. "You said that before, too. On New Year's Day."

"And I meant it then too. I was just... I needed time to figure out how to be the man you needed me to be."

"By leaving town?"

"By getting my head straight. By realizing that losing you would be the biggest mistake of my life." His hands hover near mine, not quite touching. "Let me prove it to you. Give me a chance to show you things can be different between us."

I look down at his hands, so close to mine, and feel the familiar pull toward him that's been there for years. But underneath that pull is something new; it's the knowledge that I'm carrying his child, and the weight of what that means for both of us.

"Evan," I start, then stop. I need to tell him about the baby, but the words stick in my throat.

"What?"

"There's something…" I take a deep breath, trying to find the courage. "There's something you need to know."

His expression grows serious. "What is it?"

Before I can answer, my phone buzzes on the coffee table between us. Jake's name lights up the screen, and I see Evan's eyes flick to it, his face darkening.

"Are you going to answer that?"

I look at the phone, then at Evan, then back at the phone. Jake is probably calling to check on me, to make sure I'm okay after our difficult conversation earlier. The decent thing to do would be to answer, to let him know I'm handling things.

But with Evan sitting right here, waiting for me to tell him something important, answering Jake's call feels like a betrayal of both of them.

The phone stops buzzing, and the silence that follows feels loaded with everything unsaid between us.

"Grace," Evan says quietly. "What did you need to tell me?"

I look at him… this man who's caused me so much pain and confusion, who's finally saying all the right things but might be too late. This man who's about to become a father and doesn't even know it.

"I'm pregnant," I say, the words falling into the quiet like little bombs of truth.

Evan goes completely still. For a moment, I'm not even sure he's breathing.

"What?" he whispers.

"I'm pregnant, Evan. And it's yours."

Evan's face goes through a series of expressions— confusion, shock, and then something that looks like panic. He stands up abruptly, nearly knocking over the coffee table.

"Pregnant," he repeats, his voice hollow.

"Yes."

"Mine." He starts pacing again, but this time it's frantic, like a caged animal. "Jesus, Grace. A baby?"

"I know it's a lot to process—"

"A lot to process?" He whirls around to face me, his eyes wide. "Grace, I... I came here to tell you I want to be with you, to figure us out, and now you're telling me you're pregnant?"

I can see him spiraling, the same way he did after Stefan died. The same way he always does when life throws him something unexpected.

"Evan, breathe."

"I can't... this isn't..." He runs both hands through his hair, pulling at it. "When? How far along?"

"Not sure. A month, maybe."

"New Year's," he says, more to himself than to me.

"Probably."

He stops pacing and stares at me like he's seeing me for the first time. "You've known? How long have you known?"

"Since yesterday."

"And you didn't think to call me? To tell me before I came over here talking about fighting for you and being together?"

The accusation in his voice makes me defensive. "I was trying to figure out how to tell you. This isn't exactly easy news to deliver."

"Easy?" He laughs, but there's no humor in it. "Grace, I just spent the last three weeks convincing myself I was ready to commit to you, ready to be the man you needed. And now there's a baby?"

"So that changes things?"

"Of course it changes things!" The words come out

louder than he probably intended, and he immediately looks guilty. "I mean... God, Grace. A baby. That's not only committing to you, that's... a whole life. Everything."

I feel something cold settle in my stomach. "What are you saying?"

"I'm saying I don't know if I'm ready for that." He sits down heavily in the chair, his head in his hands. "I was just getting used to the idea of being with you openly, of dealing with the family and the complications, and now..."

"Now there's an even bigger complication."

"I didn't say that."

"You didn't have to." I stand up, anger starting to override the hurt. "This is what you do, Evan. Every time things get real, every time life gets messy, you run."

"I'm not running—"

"Aren't you? Because it sounds like you're already looking for the exit."

He looks up at me, and I can see the conflict warring in his expression. Part of him wants to stay, to fight, to be the man he promised he'd become. But there's another part, the one ruling his decisions for years, that's already calculating how to escape.

"I need time to think," he says finally.

"Time to think," I repeat flatly.

"Grace, this is huge. Life-changing. You can't expect me to just—"

"What? Be happy about it? Take responsibility? Act like the man you claim you want to be?"

"That's not fair."

"None of this is fair, Evan." I cross my arms, suddenly exhausted by this conversation, by him, by everything. "But it's happening whether you're ready or not."

He stands up again, that restless energy back in full force. "I should go. I need to... I need to process this."

"Of course you do."

"Grace—"

"No." I hold up a hand to stop him. "Just go. Take all the time you need to process and think and figure out how to run away from this responsibility, too."

"I'm not running away."

"Then prove it." I meet his eyes directly. "Don't leave. Don't disappear for another eighteen months while I figure out how to handle this alone. Prove you're different now."

He stares at me for a long moment, and I can practically see him weighing his options. Stay and face the complications, or leave and avoid them.

When he starts moving toward the door, I have my answer.

"I'll call you," he says without turning around.

"Sure you will."

He pauses with his hand on the doorknob, and for a second, I think he might turn around. Might choose to fight for us after all.

But then the door closes behind him, and I sink back onto the couch, staring at the space where he was standing seconds before.

The silence feels heavier now, weighted with everything unsaid and all the ways this conversation could have gone differently. I wrap my arms around myself, suddenly cold despite the warmth of the room.

Then the tears I've been suppressing all day flow freely as I once again face the reality that I might have a baby by a man who doesn't want to become a family.

thirteen

After Evan leaves, I sit on the couch in numb silence for a long time before I remember my phone is still on the coffee table. The missed call notification glows up at me, and when I tap it, I see Jake left a voicemail.

I almost don't listen to it. Part of me thinks it would be easier to just let whatever we had fade away quietly. But something makes me press play.

"Hey, it's me." His voice sounds different than usual; less confident, more uncertain. "I know I said we should take a step back, and I meant that. You need space to figure things out, and I need to wrap my head around everything."

There's a pause, and I can hear him take a breath.

"But Grace, I can't stop thinking about you. About us. About what we had, even if it was only for a few weeks." Another pause. "I know the timing is terrible, and I know you have a lot to work through with everything. But I don't want to just disappear from your life. I care about you too much for that."

His voice gets softer, more vulnerable.

"I've been thinking about what you said, about deserving more than just stability. And maybe I'm crazy, but I think we have more than that. At least that's how it is for me." He clears his throat. "Anyway, I don't expect you to call back. I wanted you to know that stepping back doesn't mean I stopped caring. You deserve all the good things, Grace."

The message ends, and I stare at my phone for a long time afterward. The contrast between Jake's message and Evan's reaction couldn't be more stark. One man running toward me even when it's complicated, another running away.

I don't call him back, though. I can't. Not when I don't know what to say or what I want or how to untangle this mess I've made.

Two weeks later, I'm walking out of my OB-Gyn's office (which, thankfully, is not Penny's wife) with my first ultrasound picture tucked safely in my purse and my head spinning with the reality of everything. Hearing the heartbeat, seeing the tiny blob on the screen that's somehow going to become a person made everything feel suddenly, undeniably real.

I'm so lost in thought that I almost walk right into Jake as he's coming out of the bank next door.

"Grace?" He stops short, his face immediately shifting to concern. "Are you okay? You look..."

"I'm fine," I say automatically, though I probably look as overwhelmed as I feel.

He studies my face, and I can see him taking in the signs; the slight pallor, the way I'm clutching my purse, the medical building I just emerged from.

"Were you at the doctor?" he asks gently.

I nod, not trusting my voice.

"Everything all right?"

The simple question, asked with such genuine concern, nearly undoes me. It's been two weeks since we spoke, two weeks since Evan walked out of my house, and here's Jake still caring about my wellbeing like no time has passed at all.

"Yeah," I manage. "Um… routine stuff."

He knows me well enough now to see through the lie. His eyes are kind but perceptive as he takes a small step closer.

"Grace, you don't have to pretend with me. I meant what I said in my voicemail. I care about you. That doesn't just go away because things got complicated."

The mention of his message makes my chest tight. "I'm sorry I didn't call back."

"You don't need to apologize. I told you I didn't expect you to." He pauses. "But I'm glad I ran into you. How are you doing? Really?"

I look at him. This man could have easily written me off when I told him I was pregnant with another man's baby. Instead, he's standing here asking about my wellbeing with the same gentle concern he's shown since day one.

"I'm scared," I admit before I can stop myself.

"About the baby?"

I nod, surprised by how easy it is to be honest with him. "About everything. The baby, the father, how I'm going to handle another pregnancy while raising Lyndsey alone..."

"Alone?" There's something sharp in his voice. "The father isn't..."

"He's not ready," I say, which is the gentlest way I can put Evan's reaction. "He needs time to think about whether he wants to be involved."

Jake's expression darkens. "What kind of man needs time to think about being there for his pregnant... for you?"

The protective edge in his voice makes something warm unfurl in my chest. Even now, even knowing the situation between us is incredibly difficult, he's still ready to defend me.

"It's complicated," I say weakly.

"It's not complicated. Either he wants to be there for you or he doesn't. Either he cares enough to step up or he's a coward." Jake runs a hand through his hair, clearly frustrated. "Sorry, I don't mean to... it's not my place."

"It's okay."

We stand there for a moment in awkward silence, both of us clearly wanting to say more but not sure how.

"Grace," Jake says finally. "I know I said we should take a step back, and I still think that's probably the right thing. But if you need anything, at all, please call me. I meant what I said about caring about you."

"Jake..."

"I'm not trying to complicate things more. I only want you to know you're not as alone as you think you are."

The kindness in his voice, the way he's still looking out for me even though I've brought nothing but complications into his life, makes my eyes burn with unshed tears.

"Thank you," I whisper.

He nods, then hesitates like he wants to say something else. Instead, he reaches out and briefly squeezes my hand.

"Take care of yourself," he says, and then he's walking away, leaving me standing on the sidewalk with the ultrasound picture in my purse and the realization that I may have lost the best thing that ever happened to me.

<hr>

THE ANGER finally hits me a week later.

I'm standing in my kitchen making Lyndsey's lunch for school when it washes over me like a tide—hot, sudden, and completely consuming. One minute I'm spreading peanut butter on bread, the next I'm gripping the counter so hard my knuckles are white.

It's not the gentle frustration I've been carrying around for weeks, or even the disappointment that's become my constant companion. This is pure, blazing fury.

At Evan, for walking away the second things got difficult. Again.

At myself, for being surprised by his reaction when I should have known better.

At the situation, for being so impossibly complicated that even the good things in my life get ruined by it.

But mostly at the unfairness of it all.

I'm too old for this shit, especially when I'm about to have my second child with a man who can't decide if he wants to be a father. My first child already lost her dad, and now her potential stepfather, the only stable male figure who's shown genuine interest in being part of our lives, is gone because he can't commit to anything more complex than a business meeting.

Meanwhile, Jake, who could have been something real and lasting, wants nothing to do with the situation. And who can blame him? He'll have no problem finding someone without a complicated past and a pregnancy and a five-year-old and a mess of unresolved feelings.

"Mommy?" Lyndsey's voice cuts through my internal rant. "You're making weird faces."

I force my expression to relax, though my hands are still shaking slightly. "Sorry, sweetheart. I'm thinking about grown-up stuff."

"Boring grown-up stuff?"

"Very boring," I confirm, though there's nothing more interesting than the way my life is imploding.

She accepts this explanation and goes back to her pancakes, humming some song from a cartoon while swinging her legs under the table. So innocent, so trusting that her mom has everything under control.

If only she knew.

I finish her lunch with mechanical precision, my anger

crystallizing into something harder and more determined. I'm tired of being the victim in my own life. Tired of waiting for other people to decide what they want while I sit around hoping for scraps of commitment.

Evan wants time to think? Fine. But he doesn't get to keep me in limbo while he figures out whether fatherhood fits into his carefully controlled world.

After I drop Lyndsey at school, instead of going to work, I drive straight to Pierce & Pierce Enterprise. It's time for a conversation that's long overdue.

The same secretary is at her desk when I walk in, and her expression immediately shifts from professional pleasantness to barely concealed hostility.

"He's in a meeting," she says before I even ask.

"Then he can get out of it," I reply, not slowing down as I head for his office door.

"Ma'am, you can't just—"

But I'm already turning the handle, stepping into Evan's office where he's sitting across from Geoffrey and another man I don't recognize, papers spread across the conference table.

All three men look up in surprise, but I only have eyes for Evan.

"We need to talk," I announce. "Now."

Evan's face flushes. "Grace, I'm in the middle of—"

"I don't give a shit." My voice is steady, controlled, but I can see in his expression that he recognizes the dangerous calm in it. "Either we talk now, or we air all the dirty laundry in front of your business partners. Your choice."

Geoffrey clears his throat uncomfortably. "Perhaps we should reschedule—"

"That won't be necessary," Evan says quickly, standing up. "Gentlemen, if you'll excuse me for a few minutes."

The other man, someone from corporate, based on his expensive suit, looks annoyed, but Geoffrey just watches the exchange with calculating eyes. I don't like the way he's looking at me, like I'm a problem to be solved, but I don't have time to worry about that right now.

Once we're alone, Evan crosses his arms and leans against his desk. "That was unnecessary."

"Was it?" I close the door behind me and turn to face him fully. "Because you've not said a damn word to me since I told you I'm pregnant."

"I told you I needed time to think."

"About what, exactly? About whether you want to be a father to this baby? Because I have news for you, Evan, you don't get to think your way out of biology."

His jaw tightens. "That's not what I'm doing."

"Isn't it?" I take a step closer, my anger giving me courage. "Because from where I'm standing, it looks exactly like what you always do. The second something requires actual commitment from you, poof. You're gone."

"I haven't disappeared. I'm right here."

"Physically, maybe. But emotionally? You checked out the minute I told you I was pregnant."

He runs a hand through his hair, the familiar gesture that used to make me want to comfort him. Now it straight out irritates me.

"Grace, this is a huge decision. Life-changing. I can't just—"

"You can't just what? Take responsibility for your actions? Step up and be a grown fucking man?"

"It's not that simple."

"It's exactly that simple." I'm not yelling, but my voice carries the full weight of three years of frustration. "I'm pregnant with your child, Evan. That's happening whether you're ready or not. The only question is whether you're going to be part of our lives or an absent father who can't even manage the bare fucking minimum."

Something flickers across his face at that—hurt, maybe, or recognition of the truth in what I'm saying.

"I would never abandon my child," he says quietly.

"Wouldn't you?" I challenge. "Because abandoning me when things got tough? That's exactly what you do and I'm fucking sick of it."

"That's rich, coming from you," Evan says, his voice taking on a sharper edge. "You didn't seem too broken up about me needing space, considering how quickly you moved on with Jake."

The comment hits like a slap, and I feel my anger ratchet up another notch. "Excuse me?"

"You heard me. I asked for time to process everything, and within what, a few days, you were out playing house with the new guy in town."

"Playing house?" My voice is dangerously quiet now. "Is that what you think I was doing?"

"What would you call it?"

"I'd call it moving on with my life instead of waiting around for you to decide whether I was worth the effort." I take another step closer, fury radiating off me in waves. "You don't get to be jealous, Evan. You walked away."

"I didn't walk away, I asked for time—"

"Same thing, and you know it." I'm done pretending to be calm. "You want to know the difference between you and Jake? He actually wanted to spend time with me. He didn't treat me like some dirty secret he had to hide from his family."

Evan's face darkens. "So what, you went and jumped straight into bed with him to prove a point?"

The accusation hangs in the air between us, crude and insulting. I can see the moment he realizes he's crossed a line, but it's too late to take it back.

"You jealous bastard," I breathe. "You think because you finally decided you might want me, that gives you the right to judge who I spend my time with?"

"Grace, I didn't mean—"

"Yes, you did." I'm shaking with rage now. "Here's a news flash for you, Evan Pierce—until you put a ring on my finger and actually commit to something, I don't give a shit what you think about my personal life."

His expression shifts as the implication of what I said sinks in. "You did sleep with him."

"That's none of your business."

"Like hell it isn't. You're carrying my baby and you—"

"I'm carrying your baby because you couldn't be bothered to use protection on New Year's Eve," I cut him off.

"What I did after you walked out on me is my choice. You don't get to slut-shame me for moving on when you made it clear you didn't want me."

Evan's face is flushed with anger and something that looks like bitterness. "How could you do that? How could you be with him when you're pregnant with my child?"

"Because I didn't know I was pregnant yet, you idiot!" The words explode out of me. "And even if I had, you'd already made your position crystal clear by running away the second things got complicated."

"I needed—"

"Stop with the fucking excuses." I'm done with this conversation, done with his self-righteous indignation when he's the one who created this mess. "You know what, Evan? This is exactly why we've never worked. The second you have to actually fight for something, you fold. And then you have the audacity to get mad at me for not waiting around while you figure out what you want."

I turn toward the door, but his voice stops me.

"Don't walk away from me."

I whirl back around. "Watch me. I'm doing what you do Evan, and the difference is, you actually fucking deserve it, you ass!"

Swinging open the door, I storm out, and for the first time since we got together, I'm not hoping he chases after me.

fourteen

MARCH 15TH.

It's the day of Yvette's wedding and where I'm officially 12 weeks along by traditional count. Luckily the dress I'm wearing hides the slight rounding of my stomach.

I haven't told anyone other than Elizabeth, Jake, and Evan, because I have no idea what to fucking say. I'm not prepared to answer questions yet, not even to Lyndsey, yet the time is quickly approaching because I won't be able to hide it much longer.

The thought weighs heavy on me as I adjust the soft fabric of the dress in the mirror. My hands linger over my abdomen without meaning to, a gesture I find myself making more often than I realize. Protective. Secretive.

Elizabeth peeks her head into the spare room in Max and Yvette's place where I want to hide briefly, eyes immediately sweeping over me. "You look gorgeous.

Honestly, Grace, no one's going to be looking at you—they'll all be staring at Yvette. Relax."

I laugh softly, though it's tight in my chest. "That's the plan. Blend in, fade into the background."

Her smile falters a fraction as she crosses the room to fix a stray curl near my temple. "You won't fade. You never do."

I wish I could take her word for it. Despite all the bullshit, Elizabeth found her place among the family even though she didn't end up with Stefan, but my situation is so much more complicated than hers ever was.

The murmur of voices from the yard drifts through the window—everyone preparing for the ceremony to take place in a few minutes. The excitement is infectious, but I feel like I'm standing behind glass, present yet apart.

I take a steadying breath, press my hand flat against my side, and force my lips into a smile. For today, it has to be enough.

Because weddings are about beginnings. About promises and futures. And while I'm holding a future inside me, fragile and complicated, I'm not ready to share it with the world… or the entire Pierce family, yet.

Not until I know how to put words to something that still feels both miraculous and terrifying, and whether Evan is going to show up or not.

THE RECEPTION IS SMALL, intimate—only family and a few close friends gathered in Yvette's backyard strung with white lights and mason jar lanterns. Tables are set with simple bouquets, and kids chase each other across the grass while music drifts from a speaker near the porch.

It should feel warm, safe. It does, mostly. Until I spot Evan walking slowly toward me.

I've barely heard from him since confronting him in his office. A couple of texts, short and clinical:

> How are you feeling? Any nausea? You need anything?

Never anything more. Never the words I really need.

He smiles as he approaches, but it doesn't reach his eyes. "Grace. You look good."

I arch a brow, folding my arms loosely. "That's all you've got? After weeks of mostly silence?"

His jaw works, but he doesn't flinch. "I've been busy. You know how it is."

"I don't, actually." My voice is sharper than I mean, but maybe sharp is what he needs. "You pop in with these… wellness checks, like I'm some patient you're monitoring, but you don't actually *show up*. Not for me, not for Lyndsey. Just a handful of words on a screen."

"Grace—"

"No," I cut in, lowering my voice when I notice Elizabeth watching us from across the lawn. "You don't get to waltz over here in the middle of Yvette's wedding and act like we're fine. We're not fine."

He exhales, glancing away toward the tables, where Lyndsey is giggling with Max's sister Ruby over a plate of cupcakes. His features soften briefly, then tighten again. "I *am* checking in. I care about how you're doing."

"Checking in isn't the same thing as being here," I whisper, more weary than angry now. "You don't get points for asking if I've thrown up today. You either want to be part of this, or you don't."

The music shifts to something slower, couples drifting onto the makeshift dance floor. Evan watches them for a long moment, his silence louder than any argument.

And I know, deep down, that silence is my answer.

The music swells, couples swaying together beneath the string lights, laughter bubbling across the yard. I don't wait for Evan to come up with a reply—there's nothing he can say that I haven't already heard a dozen times before.

Instead, I move past him, weaving through the tables until I reach Lyndsey, who's busy licking frosting from her fingers and giggling loudly.

"Hey, sweet girl," I say, crouching down beside her. "Want to dance with me?"

Her eyes light up instantly. "Really?"

"Really." I scoop her into my arms, and she wraps her arms around my neck as I carry her toward the patch of grass serving as a dance floor. She squeals when I spin her once before settling into a slow sway with the music.

She rests her cheek against my shoulder, her laughter fading into a happy hum as I rock us back and forth. For the first time all day, the tightness in my chest loosens, replaced by something steadier. This… this right here is what matters.

When I glance up, Evan is still standing at the edge of

the crowd, watching us. His expression is unreadable—
something caught between longing and regret—but it doesn't
matter anymore. I've wasted too much of my life trying to
translate his silences and half-steps.

I close my eyes, press a kiss into Lyndsey's hair, and hold
her tighter.

He's run out of chances and I'm done being patient with
a man who refuses to grow up and face reality.

THE NEXT MORNING, sunlight spills through the blinds far
earlier than I'd like. Lyndsey is already humming in her
room, narrating some elaborate game with her dolls, and for
once, I don't mind the early start.

I linger in bed a little longer, my hand instinctively
settling against my stomach. Twelve weeks. A new beginning
I never expected, carried right here inside me. The thought
is terrifying and steadying all at once.

My phone buzzes on the nightstand. For a split second, I
brace myself for Evan's name, but it isn't him.

Jake. We haven't texted much since I ran into him, but
we stay in touch that he knows what's going on in my life,
even though we haven't discussed what happened with Evan.

> Hope the wedding went smoothly. How are
> you holding up this morning?

A smile tugs at my lips before I can stop it. Unlike Evan's
perfunctory "check-ins," Jake's words never feel like an

obligation. They're simple, but they carry weight. He actually wants to know.

I type back honestly.

> Survived. Exhausted but okay. Lyndsey's already up and singing to her dolls like it's a Broadway show.

His reply is almost instant.

> She gets it from you.

I laugh under my breath, shaking my head, and before I can talk myself out of it, I add:

> What about you? Busy day ahead?

> Not too bad. Thinking about brunch later. Want to join me? I'll make the pancakes if you bring the company.

I suck in a breath, surprised at the invitation because it has started to seem like I wasn't ever going to see him again outside of random run-ins.

I glance toward the doorway, where Lyndsey's voice carries down the hall, bright and cheerful. My chest feels lighter than it has in months.

Maybe this is what it's supposed to be like—simple invitations, steady presence, someone who shows up without being asked.

I chew my bottom lip, staring down at the message. For

months, it's felt like every man in my life either came with conditions or complications, but Jake… he just offers himself. No strings, no games, no silence I have to decode.

Even if we never become anything more than friends, even if romance isn't where this ends up, he's the kind of steady, decent man I want around Lyndsey. The kind of role model she deserves.

My fingers move before doubt can creep in.

> We'd love that. Pancakes sound perfect.

When his reply comes, it's warm enough to seep straight through the screen:

> Then it's a date. Bring your appetite.

A laugh slips out, small and genuine, and I glance back toward the hallway where Lyndsey's humming is still going strong. For once, I don't feel like I'm bracing for what comes next.

It finally feels like stepping forward instead of standing still.

fifteen

"You're glowing, Grace."

Jake's greeting is sweet, his gaze soft as he looks at me after opening his front door, and then he smiles down at Lyndsey. "You must be Lyndsey. Are you ready for pancakes?"

She nods, eyes wide. "Mom said you're her friend and I love pancakes!"

He steps aside to let us in, and Lyndsey practically bounces past him, tugging his hand. "She's... really something," I hear Jake mutter under his breath, and my chest tightens in a way I can't quite ignore.

"Only when she's fueled by sugar," I tease, giving him a small smile. He chuckles, but there's a lingering softness in his eyes as they flick back to me. I can feel the weight of the unspoken—the way he still cares, even if everything between us is tangled in complications.

"I've got the batter ready," Jake says, moving toward the

kitchen, but his hand brushes mine for just a second as he passes. My pulse jumps. "So… you've been holding up okay?" His tone is careful, like he's testing the waters.

I shrug, leaning against the counter. "Some days are easier than others. You know how it is." Lyndsey is already climbing onto a chair, impatient to start, but I can tell Jake is still watching me. There's a pause, like he's trying to figure out what he's allowed to say, or maybe what I'll let him say.

"I miss you," he admits, his voice barely above a whisper. My stomach twists. Of course he does. I miss him too, more than I'm willing to admit, but I can't let it complicate things further—not with Evan hovering somewhere in the background of our lives.

"I… miss normal," I say instead, forcing a laugh. "Before everything got so messy."

Jake nods slowly, but there's a glint in his eyes, the kind that doesn't lie. He wants more than pancakes and polite conversation. And even if it's messy, part of me wonders if maybe—just maybe—we can find a little piece of us again, even if it's only for a moment today.

Lyndsey claps her hands. "Pancakes!" she shouts, breaking the tension, and I let myself smile. For now, at least, that's enough.

"Okay, let's eat pancakes!" Jake says as he guides Lyndsey to a high chair by the kitchen island, lifting her onto it with an ease that makes her squeal with excitement.

"Wow! We don't have one like this," she says, kicking her legs.

Jake grins at her. "Well, it's a special chair so you can

watch." His voice is warm, easy, but there's that subtle tension in his shoulders when he glances at me. Like he's trying to act casual, but it's not quite working.

I lean against the doorway, watching them. Lyndsey babbles happily while Jake measures out the pancake batter. He's careful, almost protective, like he's aware she's new territory for him. It's so sweet it makes my eyes tear up slightly, which I try to hide.

"So… your favorite kind?" he asks, holding up a whisk.

"Chocolate chip!" Lyndsey yells. "And blueberries!"

Jake laughs. "Got it. Two little champions for brunch." He glances at me over his shoulder, and for a split second our eyes lock. There's a weight there—an acknowledgment that this is complicated, messy, and yet he's here, willing to try anyway.

I bite my lip, feeling a mix of comfort and longing. "You're going to spoil her," I say softly.

Jake's smile brightens, his eyes a little mischievous. "Maybe a little," he murmurs. And then, louder for Lyndsey's sake, "Alright, pancakes are coming up!"

Lyndsey claps her hands, bouncing slightly in her chair, while Jake carefully pours batter onto the griddle. I move closer, standing beside him, and he brushes past me again, this time with an almost imperceptible hesitation. Like he wants to linger, but he doesn't want to cross a line.

"You're really good with her," I say, watching how naturally he interacts.

"Yeah?" He hesitates, flipping a pancake expertly. "Good. She's special, like you." His gaze flicks toward me for the briefest moment, and my heart stutters. Even through everything, he still cares and wants me to know it.

Lyndsey giggles as a pancake flips perfectly onto her plate about thirty seconds later. "Wow! Jake's magic pancakes!"

I can't help but laugh. "Magic, huh?" I murmur, watching him beam at her.

And even though I know this is complicated, even though Evan's shadow still hangs over everything, I feel it—the pull between us, quiet but undeniable, and the possibility that maybe, for today at least, we can just... be here.

***

AFTER WE FINISH EATING, Lyndsey spots a tabby cat through the back window and begs to go outside to play. Jake opens the sliding door for her, and we watch as she chases the cat around his small backyard, her laughter carrying through the glass.

"She's got energy," Jake observes, settling onto his couch after we move to the living room.

"That's one way to put it." I sit beside him, leaving space between us but close enough to feel the warmth radiating from his body. "Jake, I owe you an explanation. About everything."

He turns to face me, his expression serious. "You don't owe me anything, Grace."

"I do." I take a breath, gathering courage. "The father of the baby... is Evan Pierce."

Jake's eyebrows lift slightly, but he doesn't interrupt.

"He's Stefan's brother. Lyndsey's uncle." The words taste bitter as I say them. "We were… involved on and off for years. Mostly in secret."

"Secret?"

"I thought Stefan didn't know, but apparently Evan told him." I keep my eyes on his face even though I want to look away the more I share. "Evan wanted to keep it quiet. Said he needed time to figure out how to tell his family, how to handle the complications."

Jake nods slowly. "And you went along with that."

"For too long. I loved him. I thought if I was patient enough, understanding enough, he'd eventually choose me openly. But every time something got difficult, he'd pull away."

"Like when you told him about the baby."

"Like every time." Heat rises in my cheeks. "I know how this sounds. Having a child with one brother, then dating the other in secret for years. It's messy and probably makes me look…"

"Human," Jake replies quietly. "It makes you look human."

His lack of judgment catches me off guard. I was prepared for questions, maybe even disgust, but not this gentle acceptance.

"When Stefan died, Evan completely shut down. Eighteen months of barely acknowledging I existed, even though we have to see each other because of Lyndsey's trust fund." I shake my head. "Then on New Year's, he shows up acting like he was ready to commit."

"That's when the baby happened."

I nod. "One night. And then when I told him I was pregnant, he panicked. Said he needed time to think about whether he was ready for 'all of this.' As if he's the only one it affects."

Jake is quiet for a moment, processing. I get up and check through the window, seeing Lyndsey has given up chasing the cat and is now making a crown of dandelions.

"I'm embarrassed," I admit after sitting back down. "By how long I waited for him. By how I kept hoping he'd change. By the whole situation."

"Don't be." Jake's voice is firm. "You loved someone. That's not embarrassing."

"Even though I was an idiot about it?"

"Especially then." He shifts closer, and I can smell his familiar clean scent. "Grace, can I ask you something?"

"Of course."

"Do you still love him?"

The question hangs between us. I want to give Jake the answer he probably wants to hear, but I owe him honesty.

"Part of me does," I say finally. "But I'm not sure that part matters anymore. Love without respect, without partnership... it's not enough. I finally understand that."

Jake nods, his gaze dropping to his hands. "I've had time to think too. About us, about what I said before."

My pulse quickens. "What do you mean?"

"I meant it when I said you needed space to figure things

out. But I also meant it when I said I care about you." He looks up, meeting my eyes. "I've been trying to convince myself that stepping back was the right thing, but seeing you today..."

"Jake."

"I miss you, Grace. I miss us. And I know the situation is complicated, I know there's a baby coming and an ex who might or might not step up, but I can't shake the feeling that we were starting something real."

"We were, definitely." The admission comes out softer than I intended.

"Then maybe we don't have to throw it away because the timing isn't perfect." He reaches over, his fingers brushing mine. "I'm not saying I have all the answers, or that it won't be difficult. But watching you with Lyndsey today, seeing how happy she makes you... I want to be part of that happiness, if you'll let me."

"What are you saying?" I ask.

"I'm saying maybe I was too quick to put up boundaries. Maybe some things are worth fighting for, even when they're complicated." His hand covers mine completely. "Maybe especially then."

I stare down at our joined hands, feeling the rightness of his touch alongside the fear of letting myself hope again.

"I don't want to hurt you," I whisper. "This situation... it's only going to get more complicated. The baby, Evan, trying to blend families..."

The fact I want Evan to step up so badly, a thought I

can't quite manage to say, but I'm not sure it matters when Jake is saying all the right things.

"Let me worry about what I can handle," Jake adds gently. "The question is, do you want to try? With me, with us?"

I look into his eyes and realize I want the possibility of joy, even if it comes with risks. He's a grown man and he seems to understand that Evan could walk back in and steal me away and wants to try anyway.

"Yes," I say, smiling softly at this man who makes me feel all sorts of wonderful even in the middle of chaos. "I want to try."

His smile is radiant. "Then that's all I need to know."

Then, he leans in and presses a soft kiss to my lips, and for the first time in weeks, everything feels possible again.

When we break apart, Lyndsey's voice carries through the back door.

"Mommy! The kitty likes me! Can we get one?"

Jake chuckles against my forehead. "Think she's going to keep us busy."

"You have no idea," I murmur, but I'm smiling as I say it.

He stands and offers me his hand. "Come on. Let's go see about this cat situation before she decides to bring it home with her."

I take his hand and let him pull me up, feeling lighter than I have in too long. Outside, Lyndsey is sitting cross-legged in the grass with the tabby purring in her lap, looking absolutely triumphant.

"Look, Jake! She loves me!"

"I can see that," he says, crouching down beside her. "What's her name going to be?"

"Princess Whiskers," Lyndsey announces without hesitation.

Jake catches my eye over her head, his expression warm with amusement. "Perfect name for a perfect cat."

And watching them together, seeing how naturally he includes her in the conversation, I feel something settle in my chest. Maybe this won't be easy, and maybe there are still difficult conversations ahead with Evan and decisions to make about the future.

But right now, in this moment, with Jake smiling at me and my daughter giggling in the sunshine, I feel like we all might actually have a chance at something beautiful.

sixteen

Jake's taillights disappear around the corner as I close the front door, still smiling from our evening together. He's been coming over more often the past few weeks, and it feels natural now. He sometimes helps Lyndsey with her homework while I make dinner, and sometimes the three of us watch movies on the couch, which feels like we're building something that feels suspiciously like a family.

I'm barely inside when there's a sharp knock at the door. My good mood evaporates when I see Evan through the peephole, his hands shoved deep in his pockets and that familiar tense set to his jaw.

I open the door but don't invite him in. "What do you want, Evan?"

"I want to talk." His voice is clipped, businesslike, but when his eyes sweep over me, they stop and widen slightly.

I'm wearing a fitted sweater that I probably should have retired a week ago, and at fifteen weeks, there's no hiding the gentle curve of my belly anymore. Not obvious to strangers, maybe, but unmistakable to someone who knows me.

"You're showing," he says, his voice softer now, almost wondering.

"That tends to happen when you're pregnant." I cross my arms over my stomach, suddenly self-conscious. "What do you want?"

He seems to shake himself out of whatever trance he was in. "I saw Morrison leaving. Again."

"So?"

"So you're pregnant with my child and you're playing house with another man."

"Stop saying that." The possessive edge in his voice makes my temper flare. "I'm not playing anything, Evan. I'm living my life."

"With him around my baby?"

"Your baby?" I scoff and step outside, closing the door behind me so Lyndsey doesn't overhear. "Since when do you get to claim ownership? You've sent maybe six texts in the past three weeks asking how I'm feeling. That's not exactly involved parenting."

"You stormed out after I told you not to walk out on me—"

"And you've been hiding ever since." I keep my voice low but firm. "You sure as hell didn't try to stop me."

Evan runs a hand through his hair, demonstrating this convo is getting to him and making him want to run, like always. "I've been trying to figure things out."

"When will you be done, huh? And what exactly is there to figure out, Evan?"

"Everything!" The word explodes out of him. "How to be a father, how to handle the family, how to deal with the fact that you're with someone else while carrying my child."

"I wouldn't be with someone else if you hadn't walked away the minute things got complicated."

"I didn't walk away—"

"You absolutely did." I'm tired of this conversation, tired of his excuses. "You know what the difference is between you and Jake? When I told him I was pregnant with another man's baby, he didn't ghost me. He asked how he could support me."

Something dark flickers across Evan's face. "How touching. And I'm sure he's been very supportive in all sorts of ways."

The insinuation makes my skin crawl. "Don't."

"Don't what? Point out that you're sleeping with him while pregnant with my baby?"

" As if you have any right to judge my choices when you abdicated all responsibility months ago."

We stare at each other in tense silence, and I can see him struggling with something. His eyes keep dropping to my belly, and there's an expression there I can't quite read.

"Grace," he says finally, his voice quieter. "That's my baby."

"Yes, it is."

"I want to be involved."

"Do you? Or do you want to control the situation without actually having to commit to anything?"

"I want..." He stops, seeming to search for the right words. "I want to do right by you. By the baby."

"What does that mean, exactly?"

"It means I don't want some other man raising my child."

There it is. The real issue. Not that he wants to be a father, but that he doesn't want Jake to fill that role.

"Jake isn't raising your child, Evan. Jake is dating me. There's a difference."

"Is there? Because from where I'm standing, it looks like he's playing daddy while I'm..."

"While you're what? Hiding? Avoiding responsibility? Sending the occasional text to make yourself feel better?"

Evan's face flushes. "I've told you I loved you. The pregnancy was a surprise. Why is it bad that I need some time to wrap my head around it? And I gave you some space, too—"

"The pregnancy was a surprise to me, also, but I couldn't hide from it like you have! And I never said I wanted space from you as the father of my baby. I said I wanted you to decide whether you were ready to commit to us as a couple." I shake my head. "Those are two completely different things."

"Maybe they don't have to be."

The words hang in the air between us, and I feel my heart skip despite myself. "What does that mean?"

"Maybe we should try again. For real this time. No

secrets, no hiding." His eyes drop to my stomach again. "We're going to be connected forever anyway. Maybe we should make it official."

"Official?"

"Move in together. Get married. Give this baby the family it deserves."

I stare at him, stunned. "Are you seriously proposing to me right now?"

"I'm saying maybe we should consider it."

"Maybe we should consider it," I repeat slowly. "Evan, do you hear yourself? You're talking about marriage like it's a business merger."

"I'm talking about doing the right thing."

"The right thing would have been not abandoning me when I told you I was pregnant. The right thing would have been fighting for us when I asked you to." I feel tears prick at my eyes. "The right thing would have been loving me enough to choose me before there was a baby forcing your hand."

"I do love you."

"No," I say quietly, a tear slipping down my cheek which I swipe away angrily. "You love the idea of controlling this situation. You love the idea of not letting another man have what you think is yours. But loving me? Actually wanting to be with me? You've never been able to commit to that."

Evan steps closer, and I can see the desperation in his eyes now. "Grace, please. We belong together. You know we do."

"Do we? Because three months ago, you couldn't handle the idea of being with me. Now suddenly you want to get married because I'm showing and Jake's in the picture?"

"It's not about him—"

"It's completely about him." I wrap my arms around my stomach protectively. "You only want what you think you can't have, Evan. That's not love. That's possession."

His face crumples slightly, and for a moment, I see the man I fell in love with all those years ago. Vulnerable, uncertain, but still too proud to admit when he's wrong.

"I'm scared," he admits quietly.

"Of what?"

"Of losing you. Of losing the baby. Of not being good enough."

The honesty catches me off guard, but it's too late for vulnerability now. Too much has happened, too much trust has been broken.

"Then you should have fought for us when it mattered," I say gently. "Instead of waiting until you had competition."

"Then what do you want from me?" The question comes out raw, desperate. "Tell me what you want, Grace, because I'm offering you everything I thought you wanted and you're acting like it's not enough."

I can hear the panic in his voice, see it in the way his hands are shaking slightly. For the first time since I've known him, Evan Pierce looks truly scared.

"You're right," I say quietly. "You are offering me everything I wanted. Marriage, commitment, no more secrets."

"Then why—"

"Because you're offering it for all the wrong reasons." I lean back against the door, suddenly exhausted. "Three years, Evan. For three years, I've begged you to choose me. To fight for us. To love me enough to take a risk."

"I am taking a risk—"

"Now you are. Because you're backed into a corner. Because there's a baby coming and another man in the picture and you finally feel like you might lose something." I shake my head. "But where were you when I needed you to take that risk because you loved me?"

His face crumples. "Grace, I—"

"Do you want to know the truth?" I interrupt, and my voice breaks slightly. "I still love you. God help me, after everything you've put me through, I still love you."

Hope flares in his eyes, and he takes a step closer. "Then—"

"But love isn't enough anymore." The words taste like dirt in my mouth. "I can't build a life with someone who only shows up when they're afraid of losing me. I can't marry someone who needed competition to realize what they had."

"That's not... I always knew what I had."

"Did you? Because your actions said otherwise. For three years, your actions told me I wasn't worth the risk, wasn't worth the fight, wasn't worth choosing openly." I wipe at my eyes, frustrated by the tears. "And now you want me to forget all of that because you're finally ready?"

"I'm here now," he says desperately. "I'm standing here

telling you I want to marry you, that I want to be a family. Isn't that what matters?"

"Why now, Evan? What changed?"

He opens his mouth, then closes it again, and I can see him struggling to find an answer that doesn't confirm exactly what I've been saying.

"Because of the baby," he finally admits.

"And Jake."

His jaw tightens. "Maybe. But does it matter why, if I'm finally ready to commit?"

"Yes," I say firmly. "It matters because this baby is going to need parents who chose each other, not parents who settled for each other out of obligation or fear."

"I'm not settling—"

"Aren't you?" I study his face, this man I've loved for so long it feels like breathing. "If I weren't pregnant, if Jake weren't in the picture, would you be standing here proposing? Or would you still be 'figuring things out'?"

The silence that follows is answer enough.

"I thought so," I whisper.

"Grace, please." His voice is breaking now. "I love you. I do. I know I've been an idiot, I know I've hurt you, but I'm here now. I'm trying to make it right."

"I know you are." And that's what makes this so heartbreaking. "But Evan, you can't undo three years of making me feel like I wasn't enough with one proposal that's motivated by panic."

"So that's it? You've made up your mind?"

I look at him standing there, this man who's been the

center of my world for so long, and I feel something inside me break and heal at the same time.

"I've made up my mind that I deserve better than being someone's last resort," I say quietly. "I deserve someone who chooses me first, not someone who chooses me when they run out of other options."

"And that's him? Morrison?"

I think about Jake's steady presence, the way he stepped into my chaos without flinching, how he makes me feel worthy of love instead of grateful for scraps.

"Jake chooses me," I say simply. "Every day, despite all the complications, he chooses me. Can you say the same?"

Evan's face goes pale, and I can see the exact moment he realizes he's lost. Not because he doesn't love me, but because he admitted he loved me too late.

"Grace—"

"I think you should go," I say gently. "We can talk about co-parenting arrangements later, but right now... I need you to go."

He stares at me for a long moment, like he's memorizing my face, then nods slowly.

"This isn't over," he says as he turns to leave.

I watch him walk away, his shoulders slumped in defeat, and I feel something fundamental shift inside me. The man I've loved for three years is finally offering me everything I wanted with him, and I'm letting him go.

"Yes," I whisper as his car pulls out of my driveway. "It is."

I press my back against the door once inside and slide down until I'm sitting, one hand cradling my belly.

And… god help me, my heart shatters because I'm turning my back on everything I thought I wanted because it's more important that I get what I actually deserve.

seventeen

I CAN'T STOP CRYING.

All morning, the tear won't stop. Even though I'm sitting in my tub trying to enjoy a quiet bath before taking Lyndsey to school, tears stream down my face in a way that feels endless. Every time I think I've gotten control of myself, another wave hits.

Lyndsey knocked on the door five minutes ago, asking if I was okay, and I managed to tell her I had a headache and needed a few minutes alone. The lie tasted bitter, but I can't explain to my five-year-old that Mommy's heart is breaking over a man who finally offered everything she wanted, just too late.

My phone buzzes on the edge of the tub. The name flashes—it's Jake, probably wondering how I am this morning. It makes me cry harder, because he represents everything good and uncomplicated in my life, and I've just chosen him over the father of my unborn child.

The rational part of my brain knows I made the better choice. Evan's proposal wasn't about love; it was about control, about fear, about not wanting to lose what he saw as his. I deserve better than being someone's backup plan.

But my heart doesn't care about rational. My heart is mourning the death of a dream I've carried for too many years. The fantasy that someday Evan would wake up and choose me, really choose me, because he couldn't live without me.

I press my palms against my eyes, trying to stop the flow of tears. This is supposed to be a happy time. I'm pregnant with a healthy baby, I have a wonderful daughter, and there's a good man in my life who actually wants to be there.

So why does doing the right thing feel like I'm dying inside?

Another knock on the door, more insistent this time.

"Mommy? Are you sick? Should I call Grandma?"

The worry in Lyndsey's voice snaps me back to reality. I can't fall apart completely. Not when she needs me to be strong.

"I'm okay, baby," I call out, though my voice sounds thick and raw. "Give me five more minutes."

I pull myself up on shaky legs and dry off, trying to erase the evidence of my breakdown. In the mirror, I look exactly like what I am: a woman who's just walked away from the love of her life because she finally learned to love herself more.

The woman staring back at me has red, swollen eyes and

blotchy cheeks, but there's something else there too. Something that looks almost like relief.

Because as much as it hurts, as much as my heart feels like it's been shredded, I'm finally free. Free from hoping Evan will change, free from accepting less than I deserve, free from the exhausting cycle of loving someone who can only love me conditionally.

I place my hand on my belly, where our baby is growing, and make a silent promise. This child will know what it looks like when someone chooses love over fear. Even if it takes me a while to stop crying about it.

TIME FLIES when you try to ignore your feelings and focus on a new relationship.

Jake and I have fallen into an easy rhythm over the past five weeks. He comes over for dinner a few nights a week and somehow manages to make everything feel normal despite the growing reminder of my complicated past expanding beneath my ribs. We don't talk about Evan, and I pretend the silence doesn't feel heavy sometimes.

At twenty weeks, I can't ignore my changing body anymore. My regular clothes officially don't fit, and the few maternity items I kept from my pregnancy with Lyndsey are either too worn out or too small. Which is why I'm standing in the local thrift store on a Saturday afternoon, sorting through a rack of secondhand maternity clothes while

Lyndsey examines a collection of stuffed animals in the toy section.

"Grace?"

I freeze at the familiar voice, my hand still gripping a blue cotton dress. When I turn around, Penny Pierce is standing three feet away with a shopping basket in her hand, her expression caught somewhere between surprise and awkwardness.

"Penny." I straighten up, suddenly hyperaware of my obvious bump beneath the fitted t-shirt I'm wearing. "Hi."

Her eyes drop to my stomach, then back to my face. "You look..." She pauses, clearly searching for the right words. "How far along are you?"

"Twenty weeks." The answer comes out steadier than I feel.

Penny nods slowly, and I can practically see her doing the math in her head. Twenty weeks means I got pregnant around Christmas, which means...

"Does Evan know?" she asks quietly.

"Yes."

"And?"

I glance toward Lyndsey, who's now having an animated conversation with a teddy bear. "It's complicated."

"Isn't it always with you two?" There's no malice in Penny's voice, only tired resignation because I'm sure she's as tired of the bullshit as I have become. "Grace, what happened? One minute you two were... whatever you were, and the next minute you're dating someone new and Evan's walking around like someone kicked a puppy."

The image of Evan hurting makes something twist in my chest, but I push it down. "He walked away when I told him about the baby. I moved on."

"He walked away?"

"He said he needed time to think about whether he was ready for all of this." I turn back to the clothing rack, needing something to do with my hands. "So I stopped waiting for him to figure out what he wanted."

Penny is quiet for a moment. "And the new guy? Jake?"

"What about him?"

"Is he okay with... all of this?" She gestures vaguely toward my stomach.

The question hits a nerve I've been trying to ignore. "Jake is wonderful. He's patient and kind and actually wants to be in my life."

"That's not what I asked."

I meet her eyes directly. "He knew I was pregnant when we started seeing each other seriously. He made that choice."

"And you? What choice are you making?"

"I'm choosing someone who chooses me back." The words come out harsher than I intended, but I'm stick of being questioned when I tried to get Evan to step up. "I'm choosing stability and kindness instead of waiting around for someone who can't commit to anything."

Penny flinches slightly. "Grace, I know Evan can be... difficult. But he loves you. Anyone with eyes can see that."

"Love isn't enough if it only shows up when someone's scared of losing you."

"What does that mean?"

I sigh, ready to move beyond this conversation. "It means he only proposed after he found out about Jake. It means he spent three years keeping me a secret and only wanted to go public when he thought he might lose me to someone else."

"He proposed?"

The surprise in her voice tells me Evan hasn't shared that particular detail with his family, although it doesn't seem like he told them I was pregnant either. "He did. And I said no."

"Grace..."

"I said no because I finally realized I deserve better than being someone's panic response." I pull a black maternity dress from the rack and hold it up, pretending to examine it. "I deserve someone who wants me enough to fight for me before there's competition."

Penny is quiet for a long moment. When she speaks again, her voice is gentler. "You're right. You do deserve that."

The admission surprises me. I was expecting her to defend her brother, to try to convince me to give him another chance.

"But Grace?" she continues. "Evan's not the only one who's scared. You've been running from your feelings for him as much as he's been running from his for you."

"That's not true."

"Isn't it? You're twenty weeks pregnant with his baby, and you're shopping for maternity clothes in a thrift store instead of letting him take care of you. You're dating another man instead of dealing with the fact that you and Evan are going to be connected forever."

Her words hit too close to home. "I tried dealing with loving him. For three years, I've tried."

"And now?"

I look over at Lyndsey, who's moved on from stuffed animals to a collection of children's books. She looks happy, content, completely unaware of the adult drama swirling around her life.

"Now I'm trying to build something healthy for my children," I say finally. "Both of them."

Penny follows my gaze to Lyndsey, and her expression softens. "She's such a good kid."

"Yeah, she is. She deserves stability. She deserves to see what a functional relationship looks like, see someone loving her mom genuinely and openly."

"And you think you can give her that with Jake?"

"I think I can try."

Penny nods slowly. "For what it's worth, I hope it works out. I hope you find what you're looking for."

There's something final in her tone that makes me look at her more closely. "What aren't you telling me?"

"Nothing. I just..." She adjusts her grip on her shopping basket. "I think both you and Evan are too stubborn for your own good. And I think that baby is going to pay the price for it."

Before I can respond, she's walking away, leaving me standing in the maternity section with a dress in my hands and the uncomfortable feeling that she might be right.

eighteen

I HAVE TO BREAK UP WITH JAKE.

The realization hits me like a physical blow as I'm driving home from the thrift store, Lyndsey chattering in the backseat about the book she convinced me to buy her. Penny's words keep echoing in my head: *You've been running from your feelings for him just as much as he's been running from his for you.*

She's right. God, she's absolutely right, and I hate her for it.

I'm not with Jake because I'm madly in love with him. I'm with him because he's safe, because he's the opposite of Evan in all the ways that should matter. But should matter and do matter are two different things, and I've been lying to myself about which category my feelings fall into.

Jake deserves better than being someone's consolation prize. He deserves better than a woman who's with him because another man broke her heart. And most importantly, he deserves better than someone who's completely in love with that other man despite all the hurt.

After I get Lyndsey settled at home with a snack and her new book, I text Jake asking if I can come over. His response is immediate and warm:

> Of course. Everything okay?

I don't answer that. I can't lie to him over text, and the truth is too complicated to explain in a message.

After the babysitter comes over, thankfully on short notice, the drive to his house feels both too long and too short. I need time to figure out what to say, but I also need to get this over with before I lose my nerve. Jake doesn't deserve to be strung along while I figure out my messy feelings.

He's waiting on his front porch when I pull up, and the sight of him makes my chest tighten with guilt. He's wearing the blue sweater I told him I liked, and there's genuine concern in his expression as I walk up the steps.

"Hey," he says, reaching for my hand. "You sounded upset in your text. Is everything okay with the baby?"

"The baby's fine." I let him take my hand, knowing it might be the last time. "Jake, we need to talk."

Something in my tone must warn him, because his smile falters. "That sounds ominous."

"Can we sit down?"

He leads me to the porch swing he installed last month,

the one where we've spent countless evenings talking about everything and nothing. The irony isn't lost on me that this is where I'm going to end things.

"Jake," I start, then stop, looking down at our joined hands. "You've been incredible these past few months. Patient and kind and understanding in ways I didn't know were possible."

"I hear a 'but' coming."

I look up at his face, memorizing the gentle lines around his eyes, the way his hair falls across his forehead. "Yes. That is, I haven't been fair to you."

"Grace, whatever this is about, we can work through it—"

"No," I interrupt gently. "We can't. Because the problem isn't something external we can fix. The problem is me."

He's quiet, waiting for me to continue, and I love him a little bit more for not trying to argue or convince me I'm wrong.

"I'm in love with Evan," I say, the words coming out in a rush. "I've been telling myself that I'm over him, that I've moved on, that he's had his final chance, but none of that is true. Not really."

Jake's hand tightens around mine for a small moment before he releases it. "I know."

The simple response catches me off guard. "You know?"

"Grace, I've known from the moment you told me about the pregnancy. The way you get that look in your eyes when you talk the situation… it's plain as day."

"Then why..." I trail off, not sure how to finish the question.

"Why did I ask for you to give me a chance anyway?" He leans back against the swing, his expression sad but not surprised. "Because I hoped maybe you'd fall in love with me. Because what we have together is good, and I thought maybe good would be enough."

"It should be enough," I whisper. "You're everything any rational woman would want."

"But you're not rational when it comes to him."

The truth of it hits me square in the chest. "No. I'm not."

"So where does that leave us?"

I look at this man who's been nothing but wonderful to me, who stepped into my chaos without hesitation, who treats my daughter like she's his own. "It leaves us saying goodbye."

Jake nods slowly, like he's been expecting this conversation. "What changed? What made you realize?"

"I ran into his sister today. She said some things that made me face some uncomfortable truths about myself." I wrap my arms around my stomach, feeling suddenly cold. "I've been avoiding my feelings, Jake, and that's not fair to either of us. No matter how much we like each other."

"And what are your real feelings?"

I take a shaky breath. "I'm terrified of how much I still love him. I'm afraid I've been punishing him for not doing things on my timeline instead of dealing with the fact that he's trying now. The reality is that I'm pregnant with his baby and I'm scared of what that means for all of us."

"Including me."

"Especially you." I turn to face him fully. "You deserve someone who chooses you first, not someone who settles for you because the alternative is too… unknown."

Jake is quiet for a long moment, staring out at his small front yard. When he finally speaks, his voice is steady but sad.

"I knew this would probably happen. I just hoped… well, that I'd have more time to convince you that what we have is real too."

"It is real," I say urgently. "Jake, what we have together is great and honest and everything a relationship should be."

"But it's not everything you want."

The gentle understanding in his voice makes tears spring to my eyes. "No. It's not, because you're not him, and I want our baby to have both parents raising it together."

He nods, then reaches over and takes my hand one more time. "Then that's what you should go for. And Grace? Don't settle for anything less than everything. You deserve that much."

The kindness in his words, even as I'm breaking his heart, undoes me completely. The tears I've been holding back spill over, and Jake pulls me into a hug that feels like goodbye.

"I'm so sorry," I whisper against his shoulder.

"Don't be sorry for being honest," he murmurs back. "Will you promise me something?"

"What?"

"Promise me you won't let fear make your decisions anymore. Whatever you decide about Evan, make sure it's what you actually want, not what feels safe or what you think you have to settle for."

I pull back to look at him, this good man I'm letting go. "I promise."

We sit together on his porch swing for a few more minutes, not talking, merely existing in this space between what was and what comes next. And when I finally get up to leave, I know I'm walking away from the easy choice toward something infinitely more complicated.

But for the first time in months, it feels like I'm walking toward the truth.

"Can I have sprinkles?" Lyndsey asks, pressing her face against the glass case at the local ice cream shop the following weekend.

"Of course you can." I'm getting a simple vanilla cone, but she's been eyeing the elaborate sundae options like they're treasure.

Once our order is complete, I find a booth by the window, and Lyndsey immediately dives into her ice cream with chocolate sauce and rainbow sprinkles. I watch her enjoy every bite, trying to work up the nerve to have the conversation we need to have.

"Lyndsey, sweetheart, I need to tell you something."

She looks up, a smear of chocolate on her chin. "What?"

"You know how my tummy has been getting bigger?"

"Yeah, like Mrs. Henderson before she had her baby." She takes another big spoonful of ice cream.

"Well, that's because I'm having a baby, too."

Her spoon stops halfway to her mouth. "Really?"

"Really."

"OH MY GOSH!" She drops her spoon entirely, bouncing in her seat. "I'm going to have a baby brother or sister?"

"Yes, you are."

"When? Can I help pick out toys?"

Her excitement is infectious, and I find myself smiling genuinely for the first time all day. "The baby should be here in the summer. And yes, you can help with lots of things."

"This is the best day ever!" she shouts, then immediately covers her mouth and giggles when other customers look our way.

"I'm glad you're excited," I say, reaching over to wipe the chocolate off her chin with a napkin.

"Can I tell everyone at school?"

"Let's wait a little bit before we tell lots of people, okay? But you can definitely talk about it with Grandma if you want."

"Okay!" She goes back to her ice cream, practically vibrating with excitement. "Am I going to be the best big sister ever?"

"You're going to be the absolute best big sister ever."

And just like that, the conversation is over. No complicated questions, no concerns about logistics. Just pure, five-year-old joy about becoming a big sister.

If only all the conversations about this baby could be so simple.

Especially since I haven't told Evan yet that I've broken up with Jake, but it's so difficult to get past how he's dealt with everything since the moment we met.

nineteen

Three weeks of thinking has brought me to this moment: sitting in my car outside work with my phone in my hand, staring at Evan's contact information.

Twenty-four weeks pregnant, and I finally know what I want to do.

I'm scheduled for another ultrasound for this afternoon; the OB-GYN said it's routine, just to check on the baby's growth and make sure everything's progressing normally. But as I was headed home to get ready, something clicked into place.

This is Evan's baby too. Whatever's broken between us, whatever mistakes we've both made, this baby deserves to have a father who's involved from the beginning. And maybe, just maybe, seeing his child on that screen will help him figure out what he actually wants.

I take a deep breath and hit call before I can lose my nerve.

"Grace?" He sounds surprised, maybe even worried. "Is everything okay? Is the baby—"

"Everything's fine," I interrupt. "I have an ultrasound appointment at four o'clock. I thought maybe you'd want to be there."

The silence on the other end stretches so long I start to wonder if the call dropped.

"Evan?"

"You want me there?"

"It's your baby, too." I grip the steering wheel with my free hand. "I know things are complicated between us, but this isn't about us. It's about the baby."

"Where?"

"The medical office on Elm Street. You've been there before with me."

"I'll be there."

"Okay." I pause, not sure what else to say. "I'll see you then."

"Grace?" His voice stops me from hanging up.

"Yeah?"

"Thank you. For asking me to come."

The genuine gratitude in his voice makes my chest tight. "You're welcome."

After we hang up, I sit in my car for a few more minutes, second-guessing my decision. Three weeks of thinking, of really examining my feelings and motivations, has led me to one uncomfortable truth: I love Evan Pierce and I always will. He's the one for me, for better or worse, and this has definitely the worst.

Not the fantasy version I built up in my head, but the real man with all his flaws and fears and inability to handle complicated emotions. The man who runs when things get difficult but who also fixed my kitchen cabinet on New Year's Day and looks at Lyndsey like she hung the moon.

Jake was right when he said I needed to stop letting fear make my decisions. I've been so afraid of getting hurt again that I've been protecting myself instead of fighting for what I actually want. And what I want, what I've *always* wanted, is a life with Evan.

But this time, I'm going in with my eyes wide open. No more waiting for him to be ready, no more accepting scraps of his attention. If he wants to be part of this and a part of our lives, he needs to show up and do the work.

Starting with today.

At home, I change out of my work clothing and into something more comfortable, trying not to overthink what's going to happen when I see him at the appointment.

Then I head to pick up Lyndsey up at school, and she's really excited when she gets into the car because I told her she could come to the appointment today to see the baby. She chatters the whole time, giggling when I tell her that Uncle Evan is going be there, too.

"Good." She grins as we pull up to the medical building. "He should meet the baby."

Out of the mouths of babes.

I spot Evan pacing by the entrance as we walk toward it, and my heart does that familiar skip it's been doing since we got together. He's wearing a dark suit that means he came straight from work, and when he sees us approaching, his expression is a mixture of nervousness and something that might be hope.

"Hey," he says quietly as we reach him.

"Hi." I adjust my grip on Lyndsey's hand. "Thanks for coming."

"Wouldn't miss it." He crouches down to Lyndsey's level. "Hey, kiddo. You excited to see your little brother or sister?"

"Yes! Mommy says I can help pick out toys and clothes and everything!" She bounces on her toes. "Are you happy, too?"

Evan's eyes flick to mine briefly before returning to her. "Very happy."

And standing there watching him interact with my daughter, seeing the genuine warmth in his expression, I remember why I fell in love with him in the first place. He's not perfect, but when he's present, *really* present, there's no one I'd rather have by my side.

Now I just need to find out if he can be there moving forward, even when things aren't perfect.

The ultrasound room feels smaller with all three of us in it. Lyndsey sits in the chair beside the examination table, swinging her legs and asking the technician a million questions about the machine. Evan stands near the wall, hands in his pockets, trying to look calm but I can see the tension in his shoulders.

"Alright, Grace, let's take a look at this baby," the technician, Maria, says cheerfully as she squirts the cold gel on my exposed belly.

Seconds later, the familiar whoosh of the baby's heartbeat fills the room through the speakers, strong and steady. Lyndsey gasps with delight.

"That's the baby's heart!" she whispers, eyes wide.

"It is," Maria confirms, moving the wand around to get different angles. "Very strong heartbeat. Let me get some measurements here..."

I watch Evan's face as the grainy image appears on the screen. His expression shifts from nervous to wonder, and when Maria points out the baby's head, arms, and legs, something in his eyes softens completely.

"Everything looks perfect," Maria says, clicking and measuring. "Growth is right on track. Baby's very active today."

As if on cue, we can see the baby moving on screen, little arms and legs stretching.

"Oh wow," Evan breathes, stepping closer to the monitor.

"Would you like to know if its a boy or girl?" Maria asks, glancing between us.

I look at Evan, then at Lyndsey, who's practically bouncing with excitement. "What do you think? Do we want to find out?"

"Yes!" Lyndsey shouts immediately. "I want to know!"

Evan's eyes meet mine. "If you want to know."

"I do."

"Great!" Maria moves the wand around, getting the right angle, then smiles as she says, "Congratulations. You're having a boy."

"A boy!" Lyndsey squeals and claps her hands. "I'm going to have a baby brother!"

I feel tears prick at my eyes as I stare at the screen. A son. Evan's son. The baby moves again, and I swear he looks like he's waving.

When I glance over at Evan, his face has gone completely soft. He's staring at the monitor like he's seeing a miracle, which I suppose he is.

"That's our son," he says quietly, more to himself than to anyone else.

Something about the way he says it—the reverence, the certainty—makes my heart clench. This is what I've been wanting to see from him. Not panic or fear, but recognition. Acceptance.

Love.

Maria prints out several pictures and hands them to us. "Baby boy Pierce, twenty-four weeks. He's looking very healthy."

After we leave the appointment, we stand outside the medical building for a moment. Lyndsey is clutching one of the ultrasound photos, chattering about all the things she's going to teach her baby brother.

"Grace," Evan says quietly. "Can we talk? Maybe after Lyndsey goes to bed tonight?"

I study his face, looking for signs of the old Evan, the one who runs when things get real. But all I see is a man who just saw his son for the first time and wants to figure out what comes next.

"Okay," I say. "Come over around eight."

He nods, then crouches down to Lyndsey's level again. "Take good care of that picture of your brother, okay?"

"I will! I'm going to put it on my mirror so I can see him every day!"

Evan stands and looks at me again, and there's something different in his expression. Something settled.

"I'll see you tonight," he says.

As I watch him walk to his car, I feel a flutter of hope in my chest. Maybe, finally, we're both ready to stop running and start building something real.

AFTER DINNER, while Lyndsey plays with her dolls in her room, I sit at my kitchen table with my phone, staring at my mother's contact. She doesn't live close anymore, having moved away for her retirement to a nice warm place, so she wouldn't have found out through the local grapevine.

I've been putting off this conversation for weeks, but after today, after seeing my son on that screen and watching Evan's reaction, I know it's time.

She answers on the second ring. "Grace! How are you, sweetheart? I was just thinking about you."

"Hi, Mom." I take a deep breath. "I'm good. Actually, I have something to tell you."

"Oh? What is it?"

"Well, I'm pregnant…"

The silence stretches so long I check to make sure the call didn't drop. "Mom?"

"Pregnant," she repeats slowly. "How far along?"

"Twenty-four weeks."

"Twenty-four weeks?" Her voice rises. "Grace, that's six months! Why didn't you tell me sooner?"

"It's complicated, Mom."

"Complicated how? Who's the father? Is it that Jake fellow you mentioned?"

I close my eyes. Of course she remembers Jake from the brief time I mentioned him since we don't talk all that often. "No. It's Evan."

Another long pause. "Evan? As in… Stefan's brother Evan?"

"Yes, Mom."

She's quiet for so long I wonder if she's trying to work out the timeline, the implications, all of it.

"Are you two together?" she asks finally.

"Not exactly. It's… we're figuring things out."

"Grace…" Her voice takes on that tone she always uses when she disapproves of what I've done, just like when I got pregnant with Lyndsey. "What do you mean you're figuring things out? You're having his baby."

"I know that, Mom."

"Does Lyndsey know?"

"Yes, of course. She's excited about being a big sister."

"And Evan? How does he feel about this?"

I think about the way he looked at the ultrasound screen,

the reverence in his voice when he said 'that's my son.' "He's... coming around to the whole situation."

"Coming around?" Mom's voice sharpens. "Grace, a man doesn't 'come around' to the idea of his own child. Either he wants to be a father or he doesn't."

"It's not that simple. It wasn't planned..."

"It absolutely is that simple, planned or not." She sighs heavily. "Honey, I know I haven't been the most involved grandmother lately, but I love you and Lyndsey. And now there's another baby to think about."

"I know."

"Are you happy? About the baby?"

The question catches me off guard. In all the chaos of the past few months, I'm not sure anyone's asked me that directly.

"Yes," I say, meaning it. "I'm happy about the baby. Scared, but happy."

"Then that's what matters." Her voice softens. "Everything else... well, everything else will work itself out one way or another."

"Will it?"

"It has to, sweetheart. You're strong, and you're a good mother. And if Evan Pierce has half the sense his brother had, he'll figure out what he needs to do."

The comparison to Stefan makes my chest tight. "Thanks, Mom."

"When can I see you? I want to be more involved this time around. I know I wasn't as helpful as I could have been when you had Lyndsey."

"I'd like that. Let me know when you will be in town and we'll have dinner. Lyndsey would love to see you."

"I will. And Grace?"

"Yeah?"

"Congratulations, honey. A baby is always a blessing, no matter how complicated the circumstances."

After we hang up, I sit in my quiet kitchen, one hand resting on my belly. My mother's right, this baby is a blessing. And in a few hours, Evan will be here, and we'll finally have the conversation we should have had months ago.

The conversation that will determine what kind of future we're going to build for our son… hopefully together.

twenty

He's late.

I check my phone for the fifth time in ten minutes. 8:23 PM. Evan said he'd be here at eight, and punctuality has always been one of his defining characteristics. The man shows up to casual dinner parties fifteen minutes early.

I pace around my living room, that familiar knot of anxiety forming in my stomach. This is what he does. He shows up when it's convenient, makes promises he can't keep, gets my hopes up and then...

The sound of a car door slamming outside makes me freeze. Through the window, I see Evan walking up my front steps, and the relief that floods through me is immediately followed by anger. I don't want to be relieved. I want to be done feeling like this every time he's supposed to show up.

I open the door before he can knock, not wanting to wake Lyndsey.

"You're late," I say without preamble.

"I know. I'm sorry." He looks genuinely apologetic, but also... different somehow. There's an energy about him I can't quite place. "I had something I needed to take care of first."

"Something more important than this conversation?"

"No." His answer is immediate and firm. "Nothing is more important than this conversation. That's why I needed to handle it first."

"You could've texted to say you'd be late."

"Yes, you're right."

Surprised at that, I step back to let him in, studying his face. He's still wearing his suit from earlier, but his tie is loose and his hair looks like he's been running his hands through it.

"Grace, we need to talk about everything. About us, about the baby, about what we both want."

"Do we?" I cross my arms, suddenly feeling defensive. "Because I've been pretty clear about what I want, Evan. The question is whether you're finally ready to give it to me, or if you're here to ask for more time to think."

"I'm not here to ask for more time."

"Then what are you here for?"

He runs a hand through his hair, and I can see him struggling with something. "I'm here because seeing our son today changed everything for me."

"Our son."

"Yes. Our son." His voice gets softer. "Grace, when I saw him on that screen, when I heard his heartbeat... I realized I've been an idiot. A coward."

"Damn right you have been."

"I know." He steps closer. "I've been so scared of screwing this up, of not being good enough, that I keep running away from the best thing that's ever happened to me."

"The baby?"

"You." The word comes out raw, honest. "You, Grace. You've always been the best thing that's ever happened to me, and I've been too afraid to admit that."

I feel tears prick at my eyes, but I'm not ready to give in yet. "Pretty words, Evan. But I've heard pretty words from you plenty of times before."

"I know. And I know why you don't trust them." He reaches into his jacket pocket and pulls out a small velvet box.

My breath catches. "What are you doing?"

"Something I should have done three years ago." He drops to one knee right there in my living room, opening the box to reveal a beautiful solitaire diamond ring. "Something I should have done when I knew I loved you."

"Evan—"

"Let me say this. Please." He looks up at me, and his eyes are glistening. "Grace, I have loved you since before I had any right to. I loved you when you were Stefan's friend, I loved you when you were pregnant with Lyndsey, I loved you through two years of stolen moments and secrets. And I've loved you every day since, even when I was too much of a coward to fight for you."

I sink onto the couch, overwhelmed.

"I know I've hurt you. I know I've let you down more times than you should have forgiven. I know I made you feel like you weren't worth choosing, when the truth is you're the only choice I've ever wanted to make." His voice breaks slightly. "I was just too scared to make it."

"Scared of what?"

"Of losing you. Of not being the man you deserved. Of our family thinking I was wrong for wanting my brother's... for wanting you." He shakes his head. "Of everything, Grace. I feared what it could mean for everything, so I chose nothing instead."

"And now?"

"Now I'm more scared of losing you than I am of anything else." He holds up the ring. "This isn't because you're pregnant. This isn't because of Jake, or because I'm backed into a corner. This is because I finally understand that loving you isn't a risk. In fact, it's the only sure thing I've ever had in my life."

Tears are streaming down my face now. "Evan..."

"I want to marry you, Grace. I want to be your husband, and Lyndsey's stepfather, and our son's dad. I want to stop hiding and start building the life we should have had all along." He pauses. "I want to wake up every morning knowing that you chose me, and go to sleep every night knowing that I chose you back."

"You're sure? You're not going to run away again?" My voice comes out as a whisper.

"I've never been more sure of anything." He reaches up

and wipes a tear from my cheek. "I'm never going to leave you again, Grace. I love you. Will you marry me?"

I look down at this man; this flawed, scared, wonderful man who has been the center of my world for so long, and I see something in his eyes I've never seen before.

Certainty. Peace. Home.

"Yes," I whisper. "I want nothing more than marry you, Evan. Fucking finally."

His laughter is loud and full of happiness as he slips the ring onto my finger. Then he's standing, pulling me into his arms, and kissing me like his life depends on it.

And for the first time in three years, I believe we're finally going to be okay.

THE SOUND of a loud noise wakes me up at seven the following morning.

I roll over in bed, momentarily disoriented, then remember. Evan stayed the night. We talked until nearly midnight, then he slept next to me, holding me in his arms until we both fell asleep. It had been wonderful and I slept deeply for the first time in a while.

But now, apparently he's awake early and being useful.

I pad downstairs in my robe to find him in the kitchen, toolbox open on the counter, working on another of the cabinet doors that's been sticking for months. He's wearing yesterday's dress shirt with the sleeves rolled up and his tie draped over a chair.

"Morning," he says without looking up from his work. "Sorry if I woke you. I wanted to get this fixed before you two got up for the day."

"You don't have to fix everything in this house, you know."

"I want to." He adjusts something with a screwdriver. "Besides, I figure I should make myself useful since I'm going to be living here eventually."

The casual way he says it makes warmth spread through my chest. Living here. Eventually. Like it's a given now, not a maybe.

"Mommy!" Lyndsey's voice carries down the stairs. "Uncle Evan's car is in the driveway!"

"He's in the kitchen!" I call back, grinning as I hear her feet thundering down the steps.

She appears in the doorway in her pajamas, hair sticking up at odd angles, and launches herself at Evan like she hasn't seen him in years instead of yesterday.

"You're here! Are you fixing more stuff?"

"Just this cabinet door." He lifts her up easily, settling her on his hip. "It was giving your mom trouble."

"Good. Mommy's not very good at fixing things." She wraps her arms around his neck. "Are you staying for breakfast?"

Evan looks at me over her head. "If that's okay with your mom."

"It's okay," I confirm. "But first, we have something to tell you."

Lyndsey's eyes go wide with excitement. "What? Is it about the baby?"

"Not exactly." I take a deep breath. "It's about me and Evan. We're going to get married."

The shriek that comes out of her could probably be heard three houses away. "What? You're getting married?"

"We are." Evan sets her down so she can bounce properly.

"That's the best news ever! Even better than the baby! Well, maybe the same as the baby." She's practically vibrating with excitement, jumping up and down while clapping her hands. "Can I be in the wedding? Can I wear a pretty dress? Will there be cake?"

"Yes to all of that," I laugh. "But slow down, we haven't planned anything yet."

She throws herself at me first, then at Evan, hugging us both with the enthusiasm only a five-year-old can manage. When she finally calms down enough to think, her expression becomes more serious.

"Evan?" she says, looking up at him with those green eyes so like mine.

"Yeah, kiddo?"

"Does this mean you're going to be my daddy now?"

The question hangs in the air, and I see Evan's throat work as he swallows. This is the moment I've been both hoping for and dreading. Lyndsey remembers a little about Stefan, but she knows the other kids at school have daddies and she doesn't anymore.

Evan crouches down to her level, his voice gentle. "I'm

going to marry your mommy, which means I'll be your stepdad. Your daddy was a very special man and nothing will ever change that."

"I know about my daddy." She nods solemnly. "Mommy has pictures of him. But he's in heaven now."

I see the mist of tears in Evan's eyes and my heart hurts for him right now even as he smiles brightly as Lyndsey. "That's right."

"So you can be my daddy now, my here daddy."

The simple, innocent way she phrases it makes my eyes burn with tears. Evan's voice is thick when he answers.

"I would love to be your here daddy, if that's what you want."

"Yes!" She throws her arms around his neck again. "You can fix things and make pancakes and read me stories."

"Well, I can definitely fix things." Evan hugs her tight. "We'll have to work on the pancakes, but I think I can manage the stories."

"Jake made really good pancakes," she says matter-of-factly. "But you're going to live here, so that's better."

Over her head, Evan meets my eyes, and I can see the humor there. I told him about breaking up with Jake last night while we were talking, and he was a bit relieved considering he'd proposed to me not knowing whether I was still seeing him or not.

"Great," he says, gaze focused back on Lyndsey. "So what do you say we make some breakfast? I can't promise pancakes, but I make pretty good scrambled eggs."

"Can I help?"

"Of course."

Watching them work together in the kitchen, Lyndsey standing on a chair beside him, chattering away while he patiently lets her crack eggs and stir, a feeling settles in my chest that I didn't even realize was unsettled.

This is what I've wanted for so long. Not just Evan, but this. The three of us together, building something real and lasting. Soon to be four of us.

My hand drifts to my belly, where our son is growing, and I think about how different his life will be from Lyndsey's. He'll have his father and mother together from the beginning, and grow up watching his parents choose each other every day.

And Lyndsey will finally have the daddy she's always wanted; not to replace Stefan, but to be the father figure she needs right here, right now.

It's everything I plan to hold on to forever, and when Evan glances up to find me smiling at them with watering eyes, he walks over, pulls me into his arms, and whispers in my ear, "I can't wait to kiss you all over later and feel everything, baby."

The call back to when he first told me he liked me makes me laugh out loud and right then, the baby kicks. I gasp, my hand flying to my stomach.

Evan immediately pulls back. "What? What is it?"

Wordlessly, I grab his wrist and press his palm flat against the curve of my belly. We both stand still, holding our breath, until—there it is. A firm, unmistakable flutter from within.

His eyes widen, then he grins. "He kicked."

"Yep," I whisper, my throat thick with emotion. "Amazing, isn't it?"

Evan's face softens in a way I've never seen before, wonder and awe breaking through every guarded wall he's ever had. He presses his hand more firmly, waiting, and when it happens again, his breath catches.

"Yeah it is." His voice is low, reverent as he leans in and kisses me softly. "But not as amazing as you, Grace."

There are no words left to say. Just the three of us standing in our kitchen, Lyndsey humming off-key as she stirs eggs, Evan's hand steady and warm over our baby, and me, caught between joy and tears.

Life didn't unfold the way I once imagined. But standing here now, I realize that doesn't matter. What matters is this moment, this truth between us, and the love we'll keep choosing—day after day—as a family.

epilogue

Christmas lights twinkle from every corner of the living room, casting the whole house in a soft golden glow. The tree is overloaded with ornaments—half of them courtesy of Lyndsey's enthusiastic decorating—and a scattering of brightly wrapped gifts crowd the base.

But all I can focus on is the weight in my arms.

Our son, Matthew, is nestled against me, dressed in a red-and-white sleeper with reindeer feet. His dark lashes rest against his cheeks as he dozes, his tiny fist curled around the edge of my sweater. Four months old, and he already feels like he's been part of us forever.

"Mommy, we can't forget to put the star on top!" Lyndsey bounces on her toes, pointing at the tree with all the authority of someone who considers herself chief decorator.

"I think that's a job for you and Evan," I tell her, shifting Matthew a little higher on my shoulder.

"Absolutely," Evan agrees, lifting her easily so she can reach after she grabs the start.

She giggles as she sets it into place, and when he lowers her back down, he ruffles her hair with a grin before glancing over at me. His eyes soften when they land on Matthew in my arms—as if the sight alone anchors him.

Adjusting the blanket tucked around our son, I breathe in that sweet, gentle baby scent. He makes a tiny noise in his sleep, and my heart aches with fullness.

The room is quiet for a moment, the four of us wrapped in the glow of the tree, and I think about how far we've come. For years I've carried the weight of being on the outside; never quite belonging, never quite certain.

But now, when the Pierce family gets together, I'm not only a guest anymore. I'm one of them. They claim me as fiercely as they claimed Lyndsey, celebrating Matthew's arrival with joy instead of questions.

Later tonight, Yvette and Max will stop by with dessert, Elizabeth promised to bring wine, and even Evan's father is coming to see the kids open a few gifts early.

Tomorrow, it'll be the whole noisy, complicated Pierce clan gathered around the table, and for once I won't feel like I'm intruding. I'll feel like I'm home.

And soon, my mother will be here, too. She hasn't met Matthew yet, and I can already imagine the tears in her eyes when she holds him for the first time. It's been a long time since she's seen me this happy, this steady, and I know she'll notice the difference right away.

I glance up to find Evan still watching me, his gaze lingering on the baby in my arms before meeting mine. There's no hesitation in his eyes anymore, no shadows of doubt. Only certainty.

When Lyndsey skips off to admire the ornaments again, Evan sits beside me and slides an arm around my waist, dipping his head close enough that his breath brushes my ear. "You know," he murmurs, a wicked smile tugging at his lips, "the best part about this time of year is all the long nights ahead that we'll have to practice making Matthew a little brother or sister."

Heat rushes to my cheeks, but I can't hold back my laugh. "You're impossible." Even though he's not at all and the idea of having more children with Evan fills my heart with such happiness.

"Maybe," he finally replies with a wink. "But I'm yours. Always."

With that certainty, my daughter humming, my son sleeping, and Evan holding me close, I finally believe in what I once thought I'd never have: a future built not on fear or waiting, but on love that shows up, day after day, exactly where it's needed.

Thanks for reading Grace's love story, finally released 12 years after the first book. I hope you love it as much as I do! <3

Join my reader's list to stay up-to-date on new releases, giveaways, events and more by clicking here!

I'll never spam you and, by joining today, you'll receive a **FREE** copy of my novella, *All the Way*.

about the author

Hey! I'm Violet Haze. I am autistic & the mother of one cool kid. I've been writing and publishing romantic fiction since late 2013. The majority of my stories are steamy romance and *all* of them are stories of true love. Happy reading!

For information on other books you can read, including links to ALL the vendors, visit my website:
www.authorviolethaze.com

Want to contact me?
Email at: violet@authorviolethaze.com

also by violet haze

If I Had You

To Break a Vow

Sugar Baby Lies

Fragments of Us

Fragments of Hope

Hungry Heart

Loving My Angel

Forever His (In the Dark #1)

Forever Yours (In the Dark #2)

Forever Mine (In the Dark #3)

To Love and Second Chances

The Seduction of Luna

Played: A Billionaire Romance

All the Way: A Dad's Best Friend Novella

Bend the Rules: A Dad's Best Friend Novella

Call the Shots: A Brother's Best Friend Novella

Deck the Halls: A Brother's Best Friend Novella

Entice His Heart: An Enemies to Lovers Novella